puzzling through the news

stories by
Pat Rushin

THE GALILEO PRESS
Baltimore, Maryland

Copyright © 1991 by Pat Rushin

Published by The Galileo Press, Ltd.
7215 York Road, Suite 210, Baltimore, MD 21212

Cover and text design by Charles Casey Martin

Publication of this book made possible
in part by a grant from the Maryland State Arts Council

Library of Congress Cataloging-in-Publication Data

Rushin, Pat, 1953-
    Puzzling through the news / by Pat Rushin. — 1st ed.
       p. cm.
    ISBN 0-913123-33-1
    I. Title
PS3568.U728P8   1991
813'.54—dc20   90-3389
                                                                       CIP

First Edition

All Rights Reserved

for my mother and father

CONTENTS

1 Man Stabbed in Heart Runs 3 Blocks

17 Speed of Light

23 Young & Attractive Suicidal Romantic Seeks Help

31 Making It Work

45 Man Breaks Hands

57 Summer Rape Tally Hits Record High

65 Election Year

81 No Visitors

95 Constrictor

109 Zoo Welcomes New Arrival

123 Baby Gets Ouchy

Man Stabbed in Heart Runs 3 Blocks

Somebody died out there.

Right there outside Morton's window overlooking Georgetown across the Potomac where he and Emily will be moving this coming weekend into a $900-a-month townhouse that Emily claims they can well afford now that she got her promotion and so long as Morton gets a decent raise this year.

"It's about time we showed some upward mobility," Emily told him last month when they looked at the cozy red-brick house on Q Street just a couple of blocks from Georgetown Med School. "A lot of doctors live in this neighborhood."

But *nine hundred dollars*. A steal, Emily called it. Almost three times the rent on their place in Rosslyn, Morton objected. "And three times the class, twice the space," Emily said. "We're going to need both if we have a baby.

"*When* we have the baby."

She kissed him. "When*ever*, I refuse to raise a kid in a dump."

"Our place isn't such a dump," Morton said.

"It's cramped, it's ugly, I killed four cockroaches in the kitchen last night: it's a dump. Come on, we're moving up in the world."

Right there, down outside Morton's window, down the street to the Rosslyn Metro Station: catch the orange line to the District and transfer downtown to the red line to Union Station and hop on Amtrak's Metroliner to New York and get off at Penn Station where it says right here on page six of the Washington *Star*, right here at the bottom of column four, how a young guy about Morton's age was stabbed for no apparent reason right through the heart right in the middle of the crowded train station by a preppie-looking kid with a 12-inch butcher knife.

And the guy lived to tell about it.

Morton folds the paper, sets it down beside the typewriter humming on the desk before him. Beyond his desk, out the window, across the river, Georgetown begins to sparkle in the heavy summer dusk. Emily should be home soon. Called around six, said she'd be working late. Had that gynecologist appointment this morning so she fell behind at the office. She hung up without saying how the appointment went.

Which means she's not pregnant.

At first, the idea of having a baby terrified Morton. A kid was a huge responsibility, he told Emily last winter, one you had for the rest of your life. Was she willing to give up her career to raise a child?

"No," Emily said. "We'll hire a sitter."

"You know how much full-time child care costs?"

"About half your salary," she said. "We can handle it."

But there were other responsibilities. You had to watch a kid all the time: it could get hurt in ways you didn't even want to think about. What if you raised it wrong? What if it turned out to be an obnoxious bully or, worse yet, some meek little sensitive creature the world would surely eat alive? What if it grew up sickly, scared, scarred for life from something you did or didn't do? What if it turned out stupid or ugly?

"A kid of ours?" Emily said. "Don't be ridiculous."

"These are things we might have to deal with."

"So we deal," Emily told him. "Day to day, like our parents did. Don't *invent* problems."

Eventually, she talked him into it.

But Morton still worries. A woman's not safe on the street after dark what with all the crazies running around. Don't worry, Emily told him when she called. She's working with Ben: he'll drive her home. Ben's got a brown belt in Tai Kwon Do. Emily's got a key ring holster full of mace. Who could threaten such a dynamic duo?

Georgetown sparkles.

Morton's going to miss this view. The place may be a dump but it's comfortable and you don't find rents like this anywhere in the Washington area except in the southeast where you don't want to live for fear you'll be walking down the street some night looking to buy a pack of smokes or something when suddenly somebody'll shove a knife in your chest.

Morton reads his lead again, suddenly rips paper from typewriter, crumples it, trashes it. He rolls in a new sheet, types the head.

STAR FALLS

The Washington *Star* is due to fold end of this week and Morton's boss at the *Post* told him okay, okay, you want out of copy editing, do me a retrospective.

"What's the slant?" Morton said.

Morton's boss rolled her eyes. "Slant," she said. "Slant. The competition's going under and he wants a slant. Do me a favor, just write it."

So he's been trying, all afternoon at the office researching and now at home looking through today's *Star* for inspiration and staring out the window feeling stupid. His boss is playing with him, he knows, just like she did last winter when he first told her he wanted to write. We hired a copy editor, she said: edit copy. But Morton kept after her until finally she said you want a chance, here's your chance, and she had him writing obituaries the rest of the week. Plenty of jokes at his expense for days after that. Then John Lennon died.

Morton loved John Lennon.

"That's feature stuff," his boss said when he asked if he could write a tribute. She smirked. "Stick to the local stiffs."

But Morton persisted until she said you write it, I'll read it, that's it, no promises.

Morton hates his boss. She must think he's some kind of ghoul. Take this guy in Penn Station he happened to read about and can't get off his mind. Guy like you or me: takes the train to work every morning, home every night; living his life day after day until one day somebody he doesn't even know kills him. Next day he shares a couple columns of wire service copy with his murderer; tomorrow he's yesterday's news. End of story. The fact that he was once alive no longer matters: not to you, not to me, not to loved ones soon enough except for a dull ache that comes and goes some sleepless night or maybe a convulsive sigh deep in the middle of a boring conversation at some cocktail party later on sometime somewhere that's misunderstood and you don't feel much like explaining anyway.

Last winter Emily stayed home from work the day John Lennon was murdered. She spent the morning listening to Beatles' albums and was still sniffling when Morton called her early afternoon to tell her the boss was giving him a shot at the Lennon tribute.

"You have to find some *significance*," she told him. "His death has to *mean* something."

"What could it mean?"

"You tell me," Emily said, voice breaking. "It's just so senseless."

Morton thought hard the rest of the afternoon, managed to decide that John Lennon's death signified the last-gasp knee-jerk of America's death-throes by the time copy deadline rolled around.

His boss grinned. "What's the matter? Couldn't come up with anything?"

"I guess it just hit me too hard," Morton said.

The next day Emily went back to work and Morton went back to copy editing.

It's dark now and still Emily's not home. He calls her office: no answer. Not to worry. Reliable man, Ben: he'll get her home all right. Morton met him at last year's Christmas party. Handsome guy, tall and trim, brilliant smile. Touch of grey across the temples, self-assured grip when Morton shook his hand. Emily said Ben was a parasitologist called back from that malaria project in Zaire to head up Acquisitions and Training.

"Which makes him my boss," Emily said.

Ben moved from circle to circle, joined any conversation in an easy, knowledgeable, charming manner: all smiles and good will and full of stories about African food and plumbing that had Emily teary-eyed with laughter.

"So, what's your line of work?" he asked Morton.

"I'm with the *Post*."

Ben raised his eyebrows, nodded. "Good paper."

"Thanks," Morton said.

"He's too good to be true," Emily said later in bed. "Intelligent, capable, sweet, funny, gorgeous. I can't believe he's still single."

"Maybe he's gay," Morton said.

Emily's eyes glittered. "What a waste if he is."

"Care to find out for sure?"

"Care to hear about it if I do?"

"Only if it's good."

Emily licked her lips, mock seductress. "With me," she said, voice low and throaty, "it's *always* good."

Morton rolled on top of her, pinned her arms, tickled her helpless.

"Stop!" she said, squirming beneath him. "You're my man, my only man."

"The best," Morton coaxed.

"You're the best," she said, gasping and giggling. "The best ever."

Morton stood up in bed, strutted unsteadily in his underwear, grinned and swaggered. "The best," he said, hands on hips. "I'm the best," he chanted over and over until Emily tripped him, wrestled off his shorts, climbed atop him and said prove it. They made love then, laughing like a couple of kids playing doctor behind the garage.

Afterwards Emily told Morton she'd been thinking about it a lot lately and she'd decided it was time for them to have a baby.

"Right now?" Morton said.

Emily smiled. "We can talk about it first if you want."

They talked about it pro and con off and on for the next few weeks. Then one cold night in early February they agreed to give it a shot.

And they've been giving it shot after shot for the past half-year without success. No physical problem with either of them. Just no luck. The thing that kills him, though: Emily got pregnant before they were married, back when they were in college together. Morton drove her to the clinic, paid for his half of the abortion.

Neither of them ever brings this up.

Morton wanders into the kitchen. Porkchops slump defrosted and draining watery blood in the sink. Maybe he should start dinner. That guy didn't even know he was stabbed at first, according to the *Star*. Just thought the small well-groomed kid in the long-sleeved V-neck sweater punched him hard in the chest until he shoved the kid away and saw the bloody knife handle growing from his shirtfront. Imagine. Should have known better.

Who wears a sweater in August?

Emily unlocks the front door, walks into the living room. Morton looks up from the typewriter.

"It's late," he says. "I was worried."

She drops her briefcase on the couch. "Jesus, what a day." Brown frizzy hair spills out of a loose bun; her white linen jacket hangs creased and rumpled from narrow shoulders. She sighs, shrugs off the jacket. "I'm beat," she says.

"Ben drive you?"

"Yeah."

"You should have invited him in for a drink."

"He had to get home." She unbuttons her blouse, damp at the armpits. "Working?"

Morton flips off the typewriter. "More or less."

"You didn't start packing?"

"Sorry, Em." Morton runs both hands through his hair. "I've been working on this thing all afternoon. Tomorrow, okay?"

Emily's jaw tightens. Morton's been saying tomorrow for the past week, she says. They're moving at the end of *this* week. "I'm so busy, I don't have time to do *any*thing." She kicks her shoes off. "This Botswana proposal's giving me a million headaches."

Morton says he's sorry, he'll start packing tomorrow, he swears to God.

Emily heads for the bedroom. "I need a shower," she says.

"Should I start dinner?"

"Let me have a shower and a drink first," she shouts. "I'll cook later."

Morton hates it when she tries to carry on a conversation from another room. Today was unbelievable, she's shouting now. She missed a staff meeting for her doctor's appointment. That looks bad, especially to those old farts who think that women are always out sick with cramps. And since she wasn't at the meeting to protect herself, she gets a million projects piled on her desk, all marked priority. Jesus.

Morton dimly understands Emily's career, tries always to express an interest. She works for a firm that puts together teams of medical professionals for government-sponsored health projects overseas: cleaning up typhoid and malaria, immunizing for measles. Morton pictures fever-blistered kids with bulging bellies and wide black eyes, staring, staring. He doesn't know. Emily keeps files of personnel they've used on previous projects; Ben's in charge of recruiting new talent: together they try to assemble a sufficiently impressive team at a cost lower than the competition's. The Agency for International Development sponsors most of the projects they work on. Safe drinking water's the big thing this year; Africa's the big place: all kinds of work up for bid now, Emily's saying. That's why she's putting in the overtime. If they get their teams together quickly, Emily says, Ben says they can sew up most of Africa.

"But the headaches," she says, "you would not believe." She walks out of the bedroom in her bathrobe. Morton appreciates the fluffy, girlish look terrycloth always gives her. "This Botswana deal, for example: you need medicals and lab people—we have that covered—but you also need engineers and building contractors with experience in sewage treatment. And they all have to speak the language."

"What's that?"

"Setswana."

"Never heard of it."

"Neither have most engineers and contractors."

She sits on his lap, kisses him. Morton tastes the stale perfume of gin.

"Ben speaks it," Emily says. "It sounds funny."

Morton nods slowly. "Botswana," he says. "There's a war going on there, right?"

"I think so. Anyway, we finished the proposal. I think we came up with a pretty good team. We'll see." She looks over her shoulder at the typewriter. "What are you working on?"

"Retrospective on the *Star*."

"They should have gone to mornings," she says. "Who reads afternoon papers?"

"I do."

"That's your job. Nobody else does." She bends closer. "Catchy title. This took all afternoon and evening?"

"Don't jinx me, Emily." Morton taps his head. "It's all up here."

Emily frowns. "Better get it on paper."

Shower hisses, typewriter hums, Morton stares at Georgetown. Emily still hasn't said anything about the gynecologist's. Give her time. Rumor around the city room says the *Post* already has hooks on twenty of the *Star*'s best writers and editors.

What's the significance?

The *Post* came out of Watergate looking like God's own word, leaving the *Star*, like so many other afternoon papers, with a dwindling readership. Traditionally, afternoon papers serve the blue collar. White collar has time in the morning for a cup of coffee, piece of Danish, and the early news. Blue collar goes off to work earlier, waits until he gets home afternoons to kick off his boots, grab a beer, puzzle through today's headlines. But blue collar work's dying out. Auto industry's laying them off. Rubber, glass, plastic industries cutting back production. You can buy your girders cheaper from Japan. Labor pool's upgrading, moving to the sunbelt. Detroit assembly-liners keypunch actuary tables on Houston terminals. Cleveland mill workers peddle insurance in Atlanta. You, too, can have a rewarding career.

Morton rips paper from typewriter again, rolls in a fresh sheet.

STAR FALLS

That guy must have known he was dead when he saw the knife sticking out. What did he think?

The shower stops. Usually Emily sings in the shower, her nasal alto bouncing old rock standards off the tiles. Not tonight. Is she thinking about the baby they haven't conceived again this month? It must be killing her. It's killing him. He was scared at first, sure, but over the months of trying he's gotten comfortable with the idea of being a father. He pictures himself rolling on the floor with daughter or son, showing her how to throw a ball, teaching him to count his toes. His heart warms and aches at the same time.

Emily comes out of the bathroom toweling her hair. "I don't hear any typing," she says.

"I'm thinking."

She comes up behind him, leans on his shoulders, shakes her hair: sweet shampoo fragrance spatters gooseflesh down his neck.

"Don't think," she says. "Write." She drapes the towel over his head. "I'm making myself a drink. Want one?"

The weirdest part of the story is that after the guy got stabbed, after he pushed the kid away and *saw* he'd been stabbed, he held on to the handle of the knife and started running. Running, up out of the train station and onto the street, blood pumping, running, as if to stop running were to die. Which may well have been the case. A police cruiser caught up with him three blocks from Penn Station: cops made him lie down on the dirty sidewalk, listened to his strange, choking story. And, story finished, he *did* die, right there on the street amid a mob of gawkers. Autopsy showed the knife had pierced his right ventricle. Should have died instantly, medical examiner said: just one of those freak cases, one for the books.

Emily comes out of the kitchen with two gin-and-tonics, gives one to Morton. He prefers scotch in the evening.

"Sit with me a second," she says.

Morton flips off the typewriter, lets her lead him to the sofa. She holds his hand, sips her drink, stares into it.

"I'm not pregnant," she says.

Morton nods. "What did the doctor say?"

"Same as last time. I'm okay, you're okay, I'm just late again, that's all. I asked was it wishful thinking or what. She said maybe I'm trying too hard, thinking about it too much. I told her I wasn't thinking about it much at all, I'm too busy thinking about work. She said maybe that's the problem, you need to relax. I said I don't have *time* to relax now, maybe next week. She said then maybe next week you'll get your period." Emily lets go of his hand, stirs her drink with her little finger. "That bitch is beginning to get on my nerves."

Morton puts his arm around her. "Don't worry, we'll get pregnant."

"Sooner or later." She sucks her little finger, pulls her lower lip into a thoughtful pout. "According to the doctor, anyway."

"Did you ask her about fertility drugs?"

"Forget it, Morton. I don't want to give birth to a litter."

"You *said* you'd ask. What's wrong with just *asking?*"

"I'm tired," Emily says. "I don't want to argue." She stretches, rubs her neck. "Probably just as well I'm *not* pregnant. I couldn't deal with morning sickness right now."

Morton looks at her.

"Come on," she says, "don't give me those puppy dog eyes."

"I just thought it wouldn't hurt to ask."

"Look," Emily says. She takes a deep breath, rubs his leg nervously. "I've been thinking, Morton, and the more I think about it the more I think maybe now isn't such a good time for me to get pregnant anyway. Now just wait. Let me finish. People at work have been telling me what a problem it is finding good child care. There's all kinds of cases of abuse and neglect, you don't know who to trust."

Her voice rises, words spill out. The more she thinks about it, the more she's starting to see how unfair it is to hand a fresh-born infant over to a sitter you *can* trust, even: unfair to both mother and child at a time when bonding is so important. Ben says a couple of years from now she'd be able to take a leave of absence at half pay, do some consulting work at home maybe, but now just isn't a good time.

Morton squints. "You don't want a baby?"

"I want a baby," Emily says. "I'm just talking about *timing.*"

Morton shakes his head. It's not registering. "All these problems," he says, "we've talked about these before. This isn't anything new."

"Plus the first year of life is unbelievably demanding. You end up losing a lot of sleep, you're up nights walking the floors with a crying baby."

"I know," Morton says. "I'll help, I'll walk the floors."

"I've just been thinking," Emily says. "It's a lot to deal with, that's all, and things are going to get even more hectic at work in the next year. Ben says—"

"Who asked him?" Morton says. "What does Ben know? *I'll* stay home. I'll quit my job and take care of our baby."

A muscle jumps in Emily's neck. "I'm serious, Morton."

"So am I," he says, and as he says it he realizes he is.

It's simple. Emily earns more than he does, Emily likes her job more than he likes his, Emily's got a chance to go places in her career: let *Morton* raise their kid.

Emily shakes her head. "Just like John Lennon, huh?"

"Why not?"

"It won't work. We need your income."

"Hey!" He grabs her knee. "Maybe my boss can give *me* some part-time work at home. All I need is a word processor with a phone hook-up." He pictures himself teaching his baby to rattle a rattle, crawl, do somersaults. "And we don't have to move to

Georgetown, do we? We could save a lot there. We could find a nice place in Fairfax or Tacoma Park or somewhere a lot cheaper."

Emily rubs her eyes.

"What do you think?" Morton says. "I think it's a great idea, it's perfect. I'll tell you the truth," he says, ducking his head and laughing, "I'm a little sick of my job anyway."

Emily covers her face. Her shoulders begin to tremble.

"Emily?"

She looks up. She's crying. "Today was awful," she says, voice shaking and nasal. "I'm tired, I have a million things on my mind, I want a baby just as much as you do, *more* even, but something's wrong, I can't get pregnant, and all I'm saying is even if I do I don't know if I can handle it. That's all I'm saying, Morton."

"Hey," he says softly. He tries to put his arms around her but she stiffens, stands, drains her drink in one gulp.

"I'm just tired," she says. "Give me a break, okay?"

"Okay," Morton says. He gives her a break.

Something died today, Morton types. Stops. Stares out the window. Georgetown beckons.

Somebody died, he types. Stops.

"How about a vegetable?" Emily calls from the kitchen.

"Fine."

"Cauliflower or broccoli?"

"I don't care."

She's trying to make up, he realizes. She's calmed down, put the problem out of mind: now she's ready for the snug reassurance of their daily life together. Give her a break. She has a rough day, she joins Ben for a drink or two after work, she pours her heart out in a way she somehow can't with her own husband, Ben gives her advice somehow more authoritative than anything her own husband has to say. Morton pictures Ben leaning across the table, idly stirring his Manhattan with sword-impaled cherry, arching his eyebrows, telling Emily in this voice vibrant with amused concern that yes, babies can be wonderful, but really now, Emily, let's put this in perspective. Morton doesn't want to picture more than that.

"We could have cauliflower with a cheddar sauce," Emily calls, "or broccoli with hollandaise."

"Either's fine," Morton says.

Somebody or something died, Morton types, out there beyond my window and beyond my control. That's right, out of the head and onto the page so it doesn't end up the aborted germ of an idea. They need a vacation, a trip to some tiny tropical island somewhere away from everybody. But she won't take time off from work. Maybe a weekend trip, up to the rolling Maryland hills for a picnic in somebody's horse pasture or maybe west into Virginia where they used to swim in an abandoned quarry they found when they'd only been married a year or two.

"We don't have to have a sauce if you don't want."

"Cauliflower," Morton says. "I want cauliflower."

"With the cheddar sauce?"

"Plain."

So what's the significance? For a few days I'll be anxiously aware of preppie-looking kids in subways. I'll never write. I won't care. I'll begin to resent and distrust my wife. Love will die. I'll never be a father.

"Don't let me interrupt," Emily says. She's standing in the kitchen doorway, head of cauliflower in one hand, paring knife in the other. "Plain cauliflower always tastes so *plain*." She laughs, nose wrinkling, eyes dancing. "Are you *sure* you don't want cheddar sauce?"

Morton shakes his head, stands. He walks towards her. "You do *not* want a baby more than I do," he says.

"Morton, please."

But there's no stopping him. When she turns away, he holds her arm. When her eyes mist up, he hardens his heart. Morton wants a baby. Morton doesn't care what they have to do or how difficult things will be. Morton does *not* want to move to Georgetown. Morton does *not* care what Ben thinks of anything and, as a matter of fact, Morton does *not* care to hear anything concerning Ben at all.

He's holding her by the shoulders now. She's crying again.

"Do you ever stop to think what I want?" she says.

"Yes," he says. "Yes, I do. I know what you want. I know what I want." He pulls her to him, holds her tight, head of cauliflower pinned between them, knife in her other hand held low and to the side.

"Let go," she says, but he hangs on, desperate now. He rubs her back, croons yes, yes, that's my baby, shush now, until her sobbing loosens, muscles unknot. She drops the cauliflower, leans into him, and Morton hugs her tighter and tighter, heart racing, waiting for the clatter of the knife on the floor.

Speed of Light

Things go wrong.

Take Constantine Muzhikovsky. He had everything going for him. Good law practice. Nice secluded house on the outskirts. Sweet little vegetable garden out back that brought him no end of pleasure come springtime. Handsome, devoted wife. Kids grown and gone. The way Muzhikovsky saw things, it was time to ease off and enjoy a tranquil, orderly life.

Then zap.

One night while they lay in bed watching Johnny Carson, Muzhikovsky's wife told him it was over. Johnny's last guest, a religious nut plugging a book, ranted on.

"Did you hear me?" Muzhikovsky's wife said.

"Yes," Muzhikovsy said. He stared at the glowing TV. "What," he said.

A blind man could see it, Johnny's guest assured him. The signs, the portents: all heralding the impending arrival of the blazing glory of our Lord and Savior, you bet. Johnny nodded sagely; then, when his guest wasn't looking, dropped his jaw, mugged dopey credulity.

The audience roared.

"I said I want a divorce."

Her voice sounded tinny, crackly, vaguely unreal. Muzhikovsky turned. She sat stiffly beside him, small breasts wrapped in folded arms, elbows pointing hard angles at the screen. Her narrow chin jerked; thin lips tightened.

"What?" he said.

She shook her head. "You never listen. I'm telling you I want a divorce."

Muzhikovsky opened his mouth, closed it. "When?" he said, finally, because he didn't know what else to say.

She turned her head, silver curls flashing in the television's glow. Fluorescent tears sizzled down her cheeks. "As soon as possible."

Muzhikovsky blinked. "Why?"

"I can't take it anymore. You're driving me crazy." Her voice was high and tight. "I don't love you."

Muzhikovsky felt suddenly light-headed. He stared at the glaring screen before him, tried to make sense of the dizzying rush of brilliant images. The screen flickered; the scene changed, changed again. Muzhikovsky couldn't keep up.

"Do you understand?" the voice beside him asked.

"You're tired," he heard himself say. "Get some sleep. We'll talk tomorrow."

But the next morning Muzhikovsky was awakened by the news on his clock radio, and all thoughts of last night's episode paled in comparison. It was incredible. He dressed and went to the kitchen. His wife poured his coffee, set the newspaper before him. Headlines confirmed what the radio claimed.

The speed of light had increased.

Muzhikovsky took a quick sip, scalded his tongue, scanned the details. It had been disclosed late last night. Scientists all over the world were coming up with the same results. The speed of light, until now constant at 299,792.458 kilometers per second, was speeding up: 301,561.5 k.p.s. last night, over 304,000 k.p.s. at press time. The President, awakened early this morning, had called out the National Guard to prevent rioting and looting. The pope had requested an hour of worldwide prayer.

Muzhikovsky sat stunned. His wife stared out the window. He could see the worry in her face, but mostly she was taking the news calmly. That was her style.

Muzhikovsky folded the paper neatly. "What do we do now?" he said. "Do we take it in stride or panic or what?"

His wife served him a slice of dry, burnt toast. She folded her arms, stood staring at him. Hers would be a fatalistic view, he realized. He hadn't lived with this woman for thirty years without learning her reactions. Her answer would not surprise him.

"There's nothing to do," she said. "It's over."

Muzhikovsky called his office, told his secretary he wouldn't be in.

"You have a meeting this morning," she said.

"Cancel it."

Her voice fluttered. "But it's with that Central Illuminating and Electric representative. You have a hearing next week on their proposed rate increases."

Muzhikovsky laughed bitterly. "It's over. Can't you see? It doesn't matter anymore."

He turned on the TV in the living room. Special reports filled the airwaves. At last confirmed reckoning, the speed of light had reached 311,218.725 k.p.s. Carl Sagan stood before a blackboard inscribed with the equation $E=mc^2$. He smiled reassuringly, spoke at some length—Muzhikovsky couldn't make out what he was saying: the voice crackled and buzzed—then carefully chalked a slash through the equal sign.

So much for relativity. So much for a logical, ordered universe. Muzhikovsky ran fingers through thinning hair. He could hear his wife puttering about upstairs. Closet doors opened and closed; hangers rattled and chimed. Muzhikovsky shook his head. The most invariable constant known to humankind had become subject to change, laws of physics were becoming obsolete at every turn, all of established existence was bound to fall apart about them, and his wife was housecleaning. He had to smile. She always maintained a marvelous sense of balance, duty, attention to detail: an attribute he'd always loved her for.

And she was right. Nothing to do now but go on doing what you've always done. Muzhikovsky considered weeding and watering his garden, but as he rose from his chair, the latest reading appeared on the screen: 359,028.025 k.p.s. He looked out the window, squinted at the bright, hazy sky, sat back down.

It seemed like a bad day to be out in the sun.

Morning passed quickly, the television a kaleidoscope of conflicting queries, theories, explanations. Evangelists preached apocalypse. Physicians prescribed caution. Scientists scratched their heads, shrugged, chattered helplessly of leptons and quarks and other mysterious entities of various flavors and colors. Perhaps, one physicist maintained, this was a natural electromagnetic phenomenon that occurred at regular intervals, somewhat like the earth's ice ages. Maybe, another argued, they'd been measuring wrong all along.

Who could tell? Layman and scientist alike were stumped. Anybody's opinion was worth as much as anybody else's.

Sitting, watching, waiting to see just how fast light could go, Constantine Muzhikovsky was formulating his own hypothesis. Things change. That's all. Things you count on. Things you take for granted. Things you never imagined could change. They change.

And, Muzhikovsky thought, there was nothing he could do to change this random changing. Nothing but change his attitude toward change.

Muzhikovsky's wife stood before him, blocking the screen. Sunlight streaked from the window behind her, framed her with a burnished silver nimbus.

"What are you doing?" she said.

Muzhikovsky shaded his eyes, smiled. "Nothing. Trying to take this as calmly as you, I guess."

"How are you doing?"

He shook his head. "It's not easy. You expect things to go on like always, then all of a sudden something you've always taken as given...." He stopped. She was biting her lip, on the verge of tears. "I'm sorry," Muzhikovsky said. "Since there's nothing we can do about it, I guess there's no sense dwelling on it."

She switched off the TV. Muzhikovsky caught an update before the screen winked out: 374,243.999 k.p.s. and climbing, still climbing, getting faster and faster. Where would it stop? Would it stop at all? What would happen if it didn't? Would the universe simply fibrillate itself out of existence? Who could tell?

"I'm sorry it had to happen," his wife said. "I know it came as a shock."

"Shock," Muzhikovsky echoed. "Yes."

But you couldn't lose your frame of reference, no matter what. One final measure of control. He was sitting in his own home. His garden was growing out back. His wife was at hand, talking to him, soothing him.

"I'm not just doing this on a whim," she was saying. "I want you to know that. I've thought about it for years, but there were the kids to think about. And then there was habit, too, I suppose. I always hoped things might get better."

"What?" Muzhikovsky said. She was sitting on the arm of the chair, touching his hand. Her fingers felt hot.

"Maybe I'm not being fair," she said. "I just can't go on, that's all."

Muzhikovsky stared at the blank screen. It seemed to brighten. Slowly at first, then faster and faster.

"Do you understand?" she said, gripping his arm.

He pulled his gaze from the television, looked up at her, astonished by her sudden urgency, but the glare from behind her slashed at his eyes, blurred his vision.

"My bags are packed. I've called a cab. We can work out the details later." She was crying now. "Just tell me you understand why I'm doing this."

Things were far too bright. Everything was going faster and faster. Muzhikovsky couldn't think, couldn't look at her anymore. He lowered his eyes, blinked.

"Doing what?" he said.

Her grip tightened on his arm. He heard sobbing; his heart quickened. He patted her hand.

"Would it help to talk?" he said.

Young & Attractive Suicidal Romantic Seeks Help

"Let's make a suicide pact," she tells her lover one night just a week before he finally decides he doesn't want to see her anymore. "If we fall out of love with each other, we'll both recognize what's happening and we'll kill ourselves together."

"My little hopeless romantic," he says, rolling off her. He reaches for his cigarettes on the bedside table. "Razor blades or poison?"

"No, I mean it, a real suicide pact, an agreement that life isn't worth living without each other."

"I'm game. Where do I sign?"

"I'm serious," she tells him.

He blows out smoke, looks at her, smiles, touches her, frowns. "Don't joke like that," he says.

"Could you not smoke right now, please?" She studies a frayed corner of the pillowcase. "My allergies."

"You *are* joking, aren't you? Because if you aren't, I don't know what to say. I've never dealt with anything like this before and I don't feel qualified. If you're serious, I feel as though I don't even know you, as though I never have known you. If you're serious, you're a complete stranger. Are you really serious?"

She looks up, eyes wide, smiles slowly. She winks.

"That's not funny," he says. He stubs out his cigarette, pulls her on top of him; she lies limp in his embrace. "For a moment there, I almost believed you," her lover says.

"If you were going to kill yourself," she says to her friend from work over drinks one evening, "how would you do it?"

"I wouldn't," he says.

"I said *if*."

Her friend from work signals the bartender. "No ifs about it. I'd never kill myself. I like myself too much."

"You could like yourself and *still* kill yourself, couldn't you? Come on," she says, "use your imagination."

He raises his glass, sucks crushed ice, signals the bartender again. "Please," he says tiredly, "no dizzy discussions tonight, okay? My day has been absolute chaos, total and irrevocable insanity. I could use a normal conversation."

She stares into her glass, eyes misting. "Sorry," she whispers.

"Where *is* the service around here? A person could literally die of thirst." Her friend from work glances at her. "Oh and please, *please*, no puppy dog eyes. Be a big girl." He sighs heavily. "Valium," he says.

"Valium?"

"Valium. Lots and lots of Valium."

"That's a terrible way to kill yourself," she says, voice rising. "That's the neurotic woman's bid for attention. You take a handful of pills, leave the open bottle on the pillow next to you, then call up your ex-boyfriend and slobber and slur until you pass out and he calls 911 and they pump your stomach and shoot you full of speed and walk you around talking tough and pretending that they really care about you."

Her friend from work raises an eyebrow. "Goodness," he says. "Hypothetically speaking, I hope."

She looks down, shrugs.

He touches her shoulder lightly. "You poor thing, I had no idea, the heartless prick. Is that the story? Do you want my advice? Take your life by the lapels, young lady, and give it a good shaking. Have your hair done, a nice semi-punky fluff. Join a spa, prance around in those adorable leg warmers. Go back to school. Treat yourself to a nice sweet uncomplicated boy your own age. Have two or three, they're habit forming. Wake up and smell the coffee. Take that frown, turn it upside down. Gather ye rosebuds and live the life. At *last,*" her friend from work says to the approaching bartender. "We're devastated here, can't you see? Two more daiquiris, *schnell, schnell!*"

"I understand you're supposed to slash them vertically," the man sitting next to her on the plane says. He takes her wrist, traces his finger up a soft blue vein. "Something like this," he says, hand lingering. "That way the sucker won't clot up so easy, I guess."

His thumb grazes her palm. She takes her hand away.

"But why anybody'd bother with that when they could just blow their brains out is beyond me." He shudders, laughs suddenly. "Hell of a conversation to be having with a pretty young thing like you," he says.

"Maybe slitting your wrists is more peaceful," she says. "It gives you time to think."

"So who wants to think? Tell you what, guy I worked with, guy I took *over* from, matter of fact, he snuffed it last year. Area superintendent before me, had four major projects under him. Couldn't take the pressure, I guess. One day he's doing his job, the next day they find him hanging from an extension cord in his attic. I'm sorry, this is not a pretty story. Wife and kids and everything. Teenage daughter found him and she's doing four hundred a week in shrink bills right now."

He shakes his head, drums the armrests with his knuckles. "Pressure takes its toll, I guess. Thing is, the autopsy showed his neck wasn't broken, so you know he had to dangle there awhile, kicking and choking and twitching. *He* sure had time to think." The man next to her on the plane stops, voice tight, lets out his breath slowly. He pats her knee. "Can you tell me something? Why am I talking about something so ugly to a girl as pretty as you?"

"I don't think you'd really be able to *think* if you hanged yourself," she says. "I mean, with hanging, the body's natural will to live would take over. It's mindless. Drowning would be the same. You know, like if you tied weights to yourself and jumped in a pool or say swam out in the ocean further than you could swim back, the body would just panic for air and you wouldn't be able to think about much else, I think. Or like those people who pour gasoline all over themselves and set themselves on fire. What could they *think* about? I mean, your skin is just *screaming* at you."

"Are you all right, honey?" the man sitting next to her on the plane asks.

"On the other hand," she says, "if you just shot yourself, there'd be no time to experience the *process* of dying. One second you'd be alive, the next you'd be dead. You wouldn't be able to appreciate the *transition*. No," she says, "the best way has to be some slow but sure, relatively painless and nonviolent way." She looks at her hands; they are in her lap, clutching her skirt so that the hem rides up over her knees. She looks up. "Poison?" she says uncertainly.

The man sitting next to her on the plane stares at her legs, mouth open. He closes it, shifts in his seat, coughs, looks out the window. "None of my business, I'm sure," he says, jaw tight, "but is this supposed to be one of those cries for help that people are supposed to notice before it's too late?"

"I—"

"Because if it is, I truly wish you'd do it somewhere else. I don't know you, and you sound pretty close to the edge to me, and I'm certainly not in any kind of position to do anything for you. You got family?"

"Some," she says. "Yes."

"Good. You talk to them. You get yourself some help." He opens a copy of *In Flight*, flips pages, slaps it closed. He rubs his eyes. "I'm sorry," the man sitting next to her on the plane says, standing, "but I have to find another seat."

"I won't lie to you," her mother tells her. "There've been times I've felt I was at the end of my rope. Right after your father passed away, it's no secret, you kids had to stay with Nana and Grandpa for a while, though you were probably too young to remember."

"I remember," she says.

"Well, I don't know how. You were just a baby." Her mother gets up from the kitchen table, refills their coffee. "Then you kids were always a handful growing up, and then when your brother got in trouble, I thought I'd never bear the shame of it." She shakes her head, lowers herself slowly into her chair. "But you do."

She hands her mother the sugar. "Did you, you know, ever think that maybe you didn't want to go on?"

"Living, you mean?"

She nods, looks down at her reflection in her coffee, blows steam.

Her mother eyes her sharply. "Sweetheart, I've learned to live with what your father did to himself. He was young and troubled and overwhelmed and sick. You have to understand that and not go reaching back. That's what made your brother so heartsick and crazy all the time. Please, don't you start in too."

"I wasn't talking about *him*, Mom," she says. "I mean you. Did *you* ever feel like that?

Her mother sits back, sighs, shakes her head. "Oh, dear heart, sure I have. I remember one time when you kids pulled some awful mischief, I can't even remember what it was now—isn't that funny? But it was something awful, and I paddled each of you and sent you off to bed, and I sat right here in this kitchen for the longest time, and I couldn't stop crying, I felt so miserable. We had a gas stove then instead of this electric, and I swear I was all ready to turn on that gas and stick my head in the oven, except it had an automatic pilot I didn't know how to work, and I was afraid of blowing up the house." Her mother laughs and laughs. "That's the difference. There's plenty of times things happened where I thought what's the use, I can't face things anymore. But you do," her mother says. "You just do."

She reaches for her mother's hand, holds it.

Her mother's eyes soften. "Do you ever feel like that, honey? Is that what you mean?"

"Not exactly." She looks away. "Yes, sometimes, I guess. Yes."

Her mother pats her arm, nods slowly. "Then you know what I'm saying," she says.

"D-Con rat poison," the strange young man who answered her ad in the Personals tells her. "That's how this lady in my building did it. Only she didn't do enough of it. It ruined most of her stomach and intestines and left her brain-dead but still alive."

She swallows the last bite of her tuna salad sandwich, pushes both their plates to the side. "That's awful," she says.

"Awful stupid." He fingers the cross-shaped earring in his left lobe. "You're going to do it, do it, that's what I think. No half-way stuff. Do it big. Do it so you *know* you're doing it. Do it so *everybody* knows you're doing it. Know what I'd do? Strap myself to a 20-megaton nuclear warhead on a long-range intercontinental ballistic missile headed straight for the men's room of the Kremlin, *bam!* That's what."

Some people in the cafeteria stare blandly at him.

She touches his arm. It's long and wiry, nearly hairless, and bruised along the bicep. "Hush," she says. "You couldn't do that."

He studies her hand on his arm, chews his lower lip. "I'm glad you're a girl," he says. "The ad didn't say. I had a feeling, though." He ducks his head. "Get much action from that?"

"Social workers," she says. "Suicide hotliners."

He sneers. "Bunch of vultures."

She takes her hand back, traces a figure eight on the table top. "My father jumped from the tenth floor of a hotel," she says. She giggles suddenly, stops.

He nods. "How'd it work?"

"Perfectly."

"Yeah," he says, still nodding, eyes glassy with thought. "Yeah, that's not bad. That's something."

"I've learned to live with it."

"But hey!" he says, leaning forward. "You know what would work even better? Go sky diving without a chute. I got a friend whose brother takes people sky diving. Better yet," he says, eyes shining, "go sky diving *with* a chute and don't open it. You'd *know* you could open it any time all the way down, you'd see the ground spinning up at you, *knowing* it's going to hit you *bang* in the face if you don't pull the cord."

He slaps the table sharply. She jumps.

"See what I'm saying?" the strange young man who answered her ad says. He stares at her wistfully. "You'd have all that time to decide."

"But don't you asphyxiate before you hit the ground?" She trails her fingers down his arm, strokes gnawed cuticles. I think I read that somewhere."

"No big deal. You bring a little oxygen tank. You can get those easy. *Hey*, or you know what?"

She leans toward him. "What?"

He ducks his head, blushes, grins. "You ever hear of the Mile

High Club? My friend's brother, he says he takes some people up sometimes just so they can, you know, do it in a plane up in the sky, just so they can say they've done it there, you know?"

She nods.

"Well, say a guy and a girl, they hold onto each other and jump together, and then they go ahead and do it on the way down. And like they're daring each other all the way down to pull the ripcord, but the rule is you can't or you lose. So they're freefalling, weightless, and they're doing it, and they try to time it so they both come at the same time just as they hit the ground. Jesus," he says, face glowing, eyes wide, "wouldn't that be something?"

"It would be different," she says, "but it sounds impossible."

"It wouldn't be easy," he says. "I'm not saying it would be easy. But you have to have a positive attitude."

"But logistically, I mean, I don't—"

"Logistically shit," he says. His teeth clench, face reddens, and a vein behind his jaw throbs to the surface. "You want to do something, you do it, you *work* it. I'm not saying it works the first time. You log a lot of practice jumps. You practice and you practice until you get better and better, until you finally *can* do it. Then you *do* it," the strange young man who answered her ad in the Personals says. His nose flares; he pants sharply, takes a deep breath, lets it out slowly. "What am I talking to you for, you know? I mean, I say something would be really something and you say yeah, well, lo*gis*tically...." Tears well in his eyes. He shakes his head. "You see what I'm saying?"

"Yes," she says, hands clutching the edge of the table. "I see," she says, slowly releasing her hold. She reaches, touches his neck, feels the earring trembling atop her fingers, a vein pounding warm and quick against her palm, and his hand tightly gripping her wrist. "Yes," she says. "That would really be something."

Making It Work

Sammy made love with Emily and Emily said it was good. So Sammy made love with Emily again and Emily said it was better. Then Emily told Mary and Mary met Sammy in a bar and rubbed her stockinged foot up Sammy's leg so Sammy made love with Mary and Mary said it was fantastic. Then Mary told Kathy and Kathy told Nora and Nora introduced Sammy to Carol and Carol mentioned it to Sarah so Sammy made love with each of them and all of them said they were delighted.

Then Sammy visited his parents for dinner and Sammy's father said when are you going to settle down son but Sammy said he wasn't ready. Then Sammy's mother started crying and Sammy didn't know what to do. Sammy said what's wrong mom but Sammy's mother just kept on crying and wouldn't eat her roast beef. So Sammy said to his father what's wrong with mom and Sammy's father said ah Sammy she's going through the change and everything's a trial for her.

But Sammy's mother blew her nose in her paper napkin and told them the change had nothing to do with it. She was upset because of her only child: thirty years old with a lousy job with no future and all he wanted to do was tomcat around with tramps and worse instead of bringing home some nice young girl and getting married and raising nice grandchildren for her.

Sammy's father said she's got a point there son and Sammy didn't know what to say.

So Sammy said I'm only twenty-nine mom and I'm not crazy about working the assembly line the rest of my life either but listen: once I decide to do something I do it. I'm thinking of taking a course in computer programming or something so my future will work out okay and I'll bring home all kinds of nice girls and get married and have kids and everything but look: your idea of nice girls is not too easy to find anymore.

Sammy's father said he's got a point there dear.

But Sammy's mother said no he doesn't. Sammy just wasn't looking in the right places. You look for girls in bars and you find tramps or worse. You look for girls in the right places like in Sammy's mother's church social group for instance and you find nice girls like the daughter of the chairwoman of Sammy's mother's church social group's bake sale. Sammy's mother met the girl last week when she complimented Sammy's mother's tollhouse cookies and she was a sweet pretty nice young girl in her last year at St. Vincent's studying to be a nurse. Sammy's mother said her name is Felicia and I can call her mother and arrange a date for you.

Sammy said oh mom please but Sammy's father said it won't kill you son and Sammy's mother wouldn't stop crying unless Sammy agreed so Sammy agreed.

So Sammy's mother called Felicia's mother and they arranged a date and Sammy picked up Felicia at her apartment and she seemed like a nice young girl with long wavy blonde hair and a nice figure in a tweed skirt and a smiling face with hardly any make-up so Sammy took her to a movie he'd already seen with hardly any sex in it and then back to her apartment. Felicia said she shared the apartment with her younger sister Bainsley but Bainsley was out with this guy Roger who Bainsley said she was in love with only she hardly knew him since she just met him last week at the community college library. Felicia said it was just infatuation and she couldn't see it: Roger was a dope. But anyway Felicia and Sammy had the apartment to themselves.

Then Felicia put on some soft jazz and poured some wine and brought out a compact mirror and a razor blade and a little vial of cocaine and Sammy laughed and told Felicia how his mother told him what a sweet pretty nice young girl Felicia was and how he agreed now one hundred percent. Felicia said she heard Sammy was nice too and Sammy said yeah every mother's son is nice but Felicia said she wasn't talking about what she heard from Sammy's mother: she heard it from her sister Bainsley who heard it from her friends Carol and Sarah.

Then Felicia said let's dance so Sammy danced with her close and slow and Felicia whispered things in Sammy's ear in a voice hushed and moist so Sammy and Felicia made love on the floor with most of their clothes on.

Then a key turned the doorlatch and they jumped up and Sammy saw a young slim girl with short fluffy blonde hair watching him zip his zipper. Sammy blushed but the girl smiled and said she hoped she hadn't interrupted anything.

Felicia said just barely not. This is my sister Bainsley: Bainsley meet Sammy.

Bainsley shook Sammy's hand and Felicia said I thought you were staying with Roger tonight. Bainsley said not tonight and she kissed Felicia on the cheek and sat on the sofa.

So Sammy and Felicia and Bainsley snorted some cocaine and drank some wine and Bainsley pulled a pipe out of her purse and some hash too and they all smoked and lounged on the sofa and Bainsley talked about how happy she was to be in love: it felt so good. Felicia stretched out with her head in Sammy's lap and her eyes closed and her hair fanning out and waving to and fro to the rhythm of the plaintive tenor sax and said how Bainsley fell in love with a new man every other new moon. Sammy stroked Felicia's hair and looked at Bainsley slouched next to him with the slit in her dress riding high up her thigh and he looked away.

Bainsley said it's tough to make love work but I try at least and this thing with Roger is the real thing.

Then they drank more and smoked more and Felicia said she was tired and she led Sammy off towards her bedroom and Bainsley winked and said have fun you guys and Felicia and Sammy got into her king-size waterbed and made love again and Felicia said I like you Sammy and Sammy said I like you too and they fell asleep. But Sammy woke up in the middle of the night and heard the stereo still playing and he wondered if Bainsley had gone to bed yet or what.

So Sammy saw Felicia again and again and they made love all the time. Sammy's mother said she was so happy he was finally spending time with a nice girl and Sammy's mother and Felicia baked cookies together and talked and giggled and Sammy's father asked Sammy if they should expect an announcement soon. Sammy said you never know.

Then Sammy told Felicia he was in love with her and Felicia told Sammy she was in love with him too and Sammy said he meant really in love and Felicia said she meant really in love too and they laughed and got serious and made love and drove to the zoo for the afternoon. They took Bainsley with them and they told her they were in love and Bainsley said she was so happy for them because love was wonderful and Bainsley saw a big hairy ape at the zoo and she said it reminded her of Roger and she smiled wickedly.

So Sammy told his parents and Sammy's mother cried she was so happy and Sammy's father said I'm proud of you son. Then Sammy talked to Felicia's parents and they said they were thrilled except they asked Felicia what about Sammy's job. So Sammy enrolled in night school for computer technology and worked days at the plant and Felicia's parents announced the engagement and Sammy saw it in the paper and told Felicia it looked good and everybody was very happy.

Then Sammy was drinking in a bar after work. Emily came in dressed in a pair of raggedy cutoffs and a high-waisted leather vest tied up the front with loose leather thongs. Emily's straight black hair was braided thick down her back and she sat on the stool next to Sammy's and told him she heard he was getting married.

Sammy said that's right.

Emily said congratulations and she kissed Sammy and when she drew away her dark eyes danced.

Then Emily bought Sammy a beer and then another and when he tried to buy one for her she bought him another and said it's on me. Emily put her foot on the top rung of Sammy's barstool and she rested her elbow on her knee and Sammy saw her cutoffs were high and tight and threadbare all along the edges and Sammy said your sandal is loose and Emily put her foot on top of Sammy's barstool between his legs and Sammy tied it for her.

Then Emily said really she couldn't believe Sammy was getting married. Not Sammy. He wasn't the type.

Sammy said well I am and Emily laughed and she said congratulations again and she kissed Sammy and ran one hand up the back of his neck and held him.

Sammy said thank you. Sammy said I should get going: I have a class tonight. Emily said just one more and Sammy said okay: maybe just one more. Emily smiled and stared into his eyes. Then she said so what do you say Sammy.

Sammy said what do you mean but Emily touched him and smiled some more and said come on Sammy. You know what I mean: don't act so innocent.

Sammy said you tempt me Emily: you know that. Sammy said but I can't. I'm engaged. I'm in love. I'm doing this right.

Emily lowered her eyes and ran her tongue over her lower lip and touched Sammy again.

Sammy said don't.

Emily smiled and kept on touching him. She ran a long fingernail up the seam of his jeans and kept on smiling.

Sammy said oh Emily: I'm asking you please don't.

But Emily kept on doing what she was doing and she wouldn't stop until Sammy grabbed both of her hands in his and held them tight and told her really he was in love and he was getting married and he wanted it to work and he couldn't fool around.

Then Emily sighed and said oh okay I'm sorry and she hugged Sammy around the neck and kissed his forehead. Emily said I thought maybe we could get together again but I see now you're serious so I'll leave you alone. Emily stood then and Sammy looked up at her and Emily bent and kissed him a sweet kiss on the lips and Sammy reached up and hung onto her braid with one hand.

Then Felicia came in.

Felicia said I called you from the hospital and you weren't home so I figured you might have stopped here after work. I thought I'd drive you to class. You're going to be late.

So Sammy left with Felicia and Felicia said who was that and Sammy said an old girlfriend and Felicia said why were you kissing her and Sammy said you won't believe this. Felicia said then don't bother telling me but Sammy said no I have to. Then Sammy tried to explain but Felicia didn't respond.

They got to Sammy's school and Sammy said are you mad but Felicia wouldn't answer so Sammy said let's go home: we have to talk.

So Felicia drove them back to her place and on the way she started talking. Sammy said don't talk like that but Felicia kept on talking. When they got inside the apartment they were arguing and Bainsley and Roger were at the table eating dinner and trying not to notice so Sammy and Felicia went into her bedroom. Then Felicia accused Sammy again of being unfaithful to her.

Sammy said I can't stand it when you talk this way. You're hard and bitchy and you aren't listening. I wasn't unfaithful to you. I'll never be unfaithful to you. I love you.

Felicia said sure you love me. That's why you were kissing that woman.

Sammy said I wasn't really kissing her. She was kissing me. I was trying to resist her when you walked in.

Felicia said it didn't look like Sammy was resisting very hard and Sammy said oh you don't understand.

Felicia said I understand maybe you can't be satisfied with just one woman.

Sammy said that's not true but Felicia said don't lie to me anymore so Sammy tried to hold her. Sammy said I love you: I'm not lying. But Felicia pulled away from him and ran out of the bedroom and out of the apartment slamming the door behind her. Sammy walked into the living room and Bainsley and Roger were sitting on the sofa watching TV with the sound way up. Roger's shirt was open and he rubbed his hairy stomach and scratched his beard and looked up at Sammy and Sammy didn't know what to say.

Roger took his feet off the coffee table and smiled and shook his head and said looks like you two had a little tiff. Bainsley took her hand off Roger's leg and leaned forward and said maybe you feel like talking about it so Sammy told them what happened. Roger said don't worry about it: it's probably just that time of the month. Sammy said no it's not. Bainsley said maybe it's the pill: I told Felicia not to go on the pill because it plays hell with your moods.

Then Sammy sat down and put his head in his hands and said

he didn't know what he was supposed to do. Roger said he didn't have to do anything: Felicia would come back after she calmed down and realized how wrong she was. But Bainsley stood up and paced back and forth and told Sammy he should go out looking for Felicia right now because you never know what's going to happen.

Bainsley said I have a friend who had a sister who was going out with this guy and they got in a fight and she ran out and he didn't follow her and then my friend's sister never came back because she was driving her car and she lost control and rammed her car head-on into a semi. She was killed. The guy felt terrible and he ended up committing suicide.

So Sammy ran out of the apartment and onto the street and he didn't even know where to look but he ran around the block and saw Felicia walking very fast and he caught up with her and pulled her to him and said he was sorry and he loved her more than anything and he would never do anything to hurt her ever again. Sammy was crying and he fell to his knees and hugged Felicia around the waist and she grabbed his hair in her fists and cried and Sammy said we'll never fight like this again: I love you too much. Felicia said I love you too and I don't want to fight.

Then they fought once more and then they fought again but both times they said they wouldn't do it anymore.

Then Sammy and Felicia were sitting undressed in her bed and they were fighting. Felicia said Sammy was *too* looking at that woman in the restaurant tonight. Sammy said what woman did she mean: he wasn't looking at any woman. Felicia said oh really: what woman weren't you looking at. Sammy said he wasn't looking at every woman in the place. Sammy said I especially wasn't looking at the woman I think you think I was looking at. Felicia said which woman was that. Sammy sighed and said the one in the black evening dress with the cornrowed hair and don't even say it Felicia because I know you think I was looking at her but I wasn't. I just couldn't help noticing her: that's all.

Felicia said sometimes I get the feeling you can't help noticing every woman but me. How am I supposed to feel.

Sammy said you're neurotic. You're nuts. This jealousy thing is making you goofy.

Felicia said I want your attention: that's all.

Sammy said you have my attention. I'm marrying you.

Felicia said that's not enough. Sometimes I think you're only marrying me because you feel it's time you were married. Face it Sammy. You really don't want to get married. You're still looking around.

Sammy said no I'm not looking around. You just think I'm looking around because you're so goddamn insecure. You say you love me. Love is based on trust. Without trust love means nothing. Without trust love can't work.

Felica said what do you mean by that.

Sammy said I mean your distrust is ruining our relationship.

Felicia said you don't want to get married. I knew it. You're backing out.

Sammy said yes he did want to get married and he wanted to marry her and live with her and love her all the rest of his life but she wasn't making it easy for him. Felicia said it's not supposed to be easy. If you want it to be easy then you don't really want to marry me. Maybe you should forget about it and just do what you want and go to bed with every woman you see.

Sammy shook his head and grabbed fistfuls of his hair and said you're driving me crazy.

Then there was a soft tap at the door and it opened and Bainsley stood in the doorway and she turned on the overhead light and she was crying.

Sammy pulled the sheet up to cover himself and Bainsley said

I'm sorry but I need somebody to talk to. Felicia said what's wrong baby.

Bainsley said I'm drunk. Roger dumped me tonight and I don't want to be alone. I have a gram of coke and I want to feel better but I feel bad right now and I don't want to feel bad all by myself: I need you guys tonight. I want you to sit up with me and do coke with me and talk with me and make me feel good about myself.

Felicia said oh my poor baby and Sammy said just let us get dressed and we'll be right out but Bainsley said don't bother and she left and came back dressed in her sleeveless terrycloth robe and she climbed onto the big bed and sat between them on top of the sheets. She pulled the coke stuff out of her pocket and they snorted some lines and she hugged Sammy and Felicia around their necks and said she felt better already. Then her bottom lip puffed out and she started crying again so Sammy cut some more lines and they snorted them.

Bainsley said I can't believe he dumped me and Felicia said did Bainsley feel like talking about it.

Then Bainsley told them how Roger found out she wasn't using any artificial birth control and how she tried to tell him that everything on the market was just too unromantical or else gave you cancer or heart attacks or strokes or cramps or infections. She tried to tell him she was using the symptothermic rhythm method and how it was just as safe as a diaphragm if you used it right and that was why certain days out of the month she wouldn't make love with him because she was ovulating. She should have told him before probably because as soon as she told him tonight Roger dumped her.

Sammy said all this time and that jerk didn't even know but Bainsley said please don't call him a jerk even though maybe he is: he knew I wasn't using a diaphragm but I guess he thought I had an I.U.D. or something although he never bothered to ask. How come my love affairs never work. How come I can't meet some nice guy like you Sammy. There must be something wrong with me.

But Felicia said don't blame yourself honey. Let's face it: Roger's a sexist dope and he doesn't respect you or your body and you're better off without him. Sammy said that's right: you're a beautiful young woman Bainsley and you can do much better than Roger. Any man would be dying to have you.

Bainsley sniffed and said do you really think so and Sammy said absolutely and he touched her hand and Felicia held Bainsley's other hand and said listen to Sammy: Sammy doesn't lie.

Sammy looked at Felicia and she smiled at him.

Then Bainsley started sobbing so Felicia hugged Bainsley to her and cooed soothing words in her ear and the sheet dropped to Felicia's waist and Sammy didn't know what to do. Sammy stroked Bainsley's short fluffy hair and said it's okay baby and Bainsley turned and hugged Sammy around the neck and kissed his cheek and Felicia kissed Bainsley's cheek and Sammy kissed Bainsley's cheek all wet and salty and Bainsley kissed Felicia and Bainsley's robe came loose and Sammy saw soft roundness rising with each sob and Sammy didn't know what to do so he kissed Bainsley's neck. Bainsley turned to Sammy and kissed his lips still crying and Sammy said don't cry Bainsley but she kept on crying and Felicia started crying so Sammy hugged them both and kissed them and Felicia kissed Bainsley's hair and Bainsley clung to Sammy's neck and Sammy kissed Felicia's ear and Felicia whispered oh God and Bainsley gasped and sobbed and Sammy twitched and rolled and they all made love together and the waterbed sloshed and ebbed.

Then Bainsley rolled over and smiled through her tears and said that was beautiful.

But Felicia said I can't believe we did that. That wasn't natural. I've never even thought of doing something like that.

Bainsley said it's okay. Don't feel bad. You guys made me feel happy and nothing that makes you feel happy is unnatural.

But Felicia said the coke made you feel happy and we wouldn't have done this if we weren't so high.

Then Sammy spoke up and said don't spoil it like that Felicia. We enjoyed ourselves. I know I did and I know Bainsley did and I know you did too. I could tell. It happened. Let's at least admit it was good.

Felicia said just because it was good that doesn't mean it was right. What would our parents say if they knew. What would your mother say Sammy.

Sammy said they wouldn't understand. None of them.

Felicia said I'm not sure I understand.

Then Bainsley rubbed tears from her eyes and said I don't like you guys talking like this. You make me feel guilty. You make it seem like it shouldn't have happened. I don't want to feel guilty about this.

Then Felicia looked at Bainsley and she kissed her forehead and said you're right. You're both right. It happened. I enjoyed it. We shouldn't feel guilty about it. I guess it proves how close we are and that makes me feel good. But that doesn't mean it has to happen again.

Bainsley raised her eyebrows and said she really wouldn't mind if it happened again and she looked at Sammy.

But Sammy said no your sister's probably right Bainsley: when we talk about a thing like this we're talking the kind of thing that hardly ever works out for the better even though it might work out very nice in the short run. The thing to do is say okay: we had a good time but that's it.

Felicia agreed with Sammy one hundred percent so Bainsley said okay I guess we won't make love with each other all together again and Sammy said I guess not.

But Bainsley didn't feel like sleeping alone especially after all the excitement and Felicia said she might as well sleep with her and Sammy and Sammy had no objections so they cuddled up and kissed each other goodnight and went to sleep. Then Sammy woke up in the middle of the night and he felt a warm hand on his right leg and a soft face breathing moist against his left shoulder and Sammy didn't know what to do.

So then they all made love again anyway.

Man Breaks Hands

Thursday night man breaks hands. Friday morning Cleveland Browns orthopedic surgeon breaks bad news: second, third, fourth metacarpals in both hands; knuckles bashed all to hell. How'd man manage that?

"Fell down," man says.

Browns trainer says don't hand him that crap. Man get in fight or what?

"What," man says.

Browns coach says quit fucking around. Man'll be out most of season, could be on waivers next year.

"You need me," man says.

"Nobody needs a wide receiver with broken hands. Wise up. Tell me what happened."

Man loves coach like father he should've had. Man spills guts.

"Sweet Jesus," coach says. "Pittsburgh prime to stomp our butts Sunday and he's fucking around with phone poles. Shouldna been out drinking in the first place. Shoulda stayed home with your wife."

Man's wife was with him.

"That's awful," says coach. "You do that shit in front of your wife? That's stupid," says coach. "You're ruining your career."

Man begins to cry.

Coach comforts man. It's okay, he tells him. But listen, man better lay low awhile. Don't dress for this week's game. Don't even *come* to game. Maybe not even *next* week's game. Coach has to figure some way to tell press.

Sunday afternoon man sits in front of tube. Pittsburgh leads Cleveland 7-0. One rugged rivalry, announcer says. Cleveland stands at 2-3; Pittsburgh, Cincinnati, Houston share AFC Central lead at 3-2. One rugged division, announcer says. Man's wife sits across room paging through *Glamour*. Announcer says man's name: report just came in man broke finger in practice. Man stares at hands, all heavy plaster from fingertips to mid-forearms except for two hairy pinkies.

Man asks for beer.

Wife sets beer on arm of chair, inserts straw in bottle, rubs man's neck. "Cheer up," she says.

New report, announcer says: man appears to have broken more than one finger; exact number unknown; awaiting details.

"You didn't tell anybody how you did it," wife says. "Did you?"

Man pins beer between plaster paws, sucks straw.

"Did you?"

Man says just coach.

Wife sighs. "It'll be all over the papers tomorrow."

Halftime: 10-7 Pittsburgh. Man fumbles beer. Wife sponges man's lap.

"Did you tell anybody *why* you did it?"

Man says nobody.

Third quarter Brian Sipe gets sacked. Jack Lambert gets roughing passer call. Sipe gets concussion. Unknown how serious. Man thinks of ruined knuckles, crushed bones.

"I don't want you telling anybody why you did it," wife says. "Okay?"

"Okay," man says. "I love you."

"I love you too," wife says. "Okay."

Fourth quarter Paul McDonald filling in for Sipe throws to double-teamed Ozzie Newsome in endzone. Ball is tipped, intercepted. Pittsburgh wins 13-7.

"I have to get out of here," man says.

Wife wants to know where to. Man says corner bar. Wife says she'll join him. Man says he'd rather be alone.

"You can't do anything alone," says wife.

Place is dim, smoky, near empty. Dusty softball and bowling trophies guard shelf over green vinyl booths lining right side; scarred walnut bar lines left. Houston-Seattle game blares tinny play-by-plays from tube at far end of bar. Man and wife sit at near end next to couple talking football: husky guy, flat-faced, thin hair combed across balding dome; pale woman, red hair permed tight, pink lipstick smeared beneath bulbed nose. Guy's talking about dumb call, third and five you pass. Woman says listen to the armchair quarterback. Guy says shut up, Edna, what the hell do *you* know. Edna says twice as much as *you*, Howard. Howard says ah shut up.

Man holds casts out of sight in lap.

"I need a drink," says wife.

Man looks down bar. Bartender's at far end leaning heavy belly against bartop, smiling at blonde girl in jeans and flannel shirt. Blonde girl talks. Bartender laughs. Ken Stabler connects with wide receiver Ken Burrough for touchdown.

"Damn," says man.

"Hey Hank," wife calls. "How about some service?"

Bartender hustles down, makes big fuss. Where *was* man today. Brownies missed him god*damn*. What happened? Man shushes bartender, glances at couple next to him—still arguing—

whispers he doesn't feel like being recognized today. Ah, sure thing, bartender rasps. How about them fingers?

"How about a scotch on the rocks," says wife. "And give this man a draft with a straw."

Bartender blinks. Man clunks casts on bar.

"Holy shit," bartender breathes. "What did you *do*?"

Man glances at wife. "Don't ask."

Howard nudges Edna. "Hell of a break," he says. "How do you wipe your ass?"

"Don't ask," says man.

Howard laughs. "C'mon, how'd you do it?"

"Car accident," says wife.

Howard snorts. "Bullshit."

"Don't be so crude," says Edna. "Maybe it's none of your business."

Howard says it's none of Edna's business whose business it is.

"Don't mind him," says Edna. "He gets obnoxious when he's drunk. You get in a fight?"

"Yeah," man says.

"I do not," says Howard.

"A fight?" says bartender. "Holy shit. Who with?"

Man says don't ask.

Wife says how about those drinks, Hank, huh? Hank says sure thing. Man sucks beer, hears Edna say if he doesn't want to tell you he doesn't want to tell you, don't be so goddamn obnoxious. Howard says *he's* not the obnoxious one. If Howard broke his hands he'd sure as hell tell people *exactly* how it happened, be it fighting, fucking, or farting. Edna says okay, okay, just shut up for godsakes. Howard says he'll shut up when he feels like it. Earl Campbell plunges in from one-yard line. Edna says will you look at the thighs on him.

"Let's sit over in a booth," wife says.

"Later," says man. "I want to watch the game."

Man sucks beer. Orders another. Sucks more beer. Orders another beer, another straw. Sucks. Wife goes to ladies room. Stabler scores on 32-yard pass to Dave Casper. Howard slaps man on back.

"Now that's a play, ain't it buddy?"

"Sure is," says man.

"I mean that is one hell of a play."

Edna elbows bar, chin in hand. "It worked, didn't it?"

Howard glares at her. "Who asked you?" he says. "What do you know?" he says. "Takes a *man* to know what the hell's a play and what ain't." Howard slaps man's back again. "Women don't know shit about football."

"Don't touch me anymore," man says.

Howard pulls back. "Whats wrong with *you?*"

"Howard," says Edna. "Leave the man alone and just shut up."

Howard spins around, grabs Edna's arm, says if Edna tells him to shut up again she'll be sorry. Edna says he's hurting her. Howard says he means it, enough's enough so just lay off. Edna's pink mouth twists and works. Let go you bastard, she says. Howard says fuck you.

Man stands.

Man tells Howard that one does not speak to a woman in such a manner; neither does one threaten a woman with violence; *never* does one touch a woman in such a way as to hurt her. Man suggests Howard release Edna before man kicks living breathing shit out of Howard's stupid ass.

Howard lets go, says why doesn't man mind own business, is man supposed to be some kind of badass? Man raises casts. Edna rubs arm, says that's it, picks up purse and heads out door. Howard yells good riddance bitch. Bartender rushes down says no trouble please. Man says no trouble, just difference of opinion. Bartender tells Howard why doesn't he go after Edna. Howard says not a chance, he wants another drink.

Man picks up beer between casts, heads for far end of bar. Halfway there mug slips, spills, shatters shards and foam all over floor. Howard claps. Man blushes. Bartender says don't worry about it. Man sits one empty stool away from blonde girl in flannel shirt.

"Kind of clumsy these days," man says.

Blonde girl smiles, looks up at game. Man can't help noticing: wide eyes, wispy short tomboyish hair, fresh face. Twenty, twenty-one tops. Can't help noticing sleek flex of haunch in tight denim when she jumps as Stabler avoids getting sacked with outlet pass to Campbell who puts head down and rams linebacker, dragging three tacklers five extra yards.

"Tough to stop that," she says. "Houston's looking good."

"Better than last week."

"Stabler's passing was off."

"He got killed. One for seven."

Can't help noticing smooth swell of smallish breasts rising as girl swivels toward him.

"One for six," she says. "This game should boost his confidence. I like Stabler."

"Me too. He never gives up."

She nods towards far end of bar. "I saw what you did. I like that. I hate men who bully women. I had a boyfriend once who bullied me even though he never really hit me. I like how you stood up for that woman and I promise I won't ask about your hands if you don't want."

"I hate bullies too," man says.

Girl stares at casts. "Where's your girlfriend?"

"Wife," says man. "She's in the rest room. She takes a long time."

"A lot of women do," girl says. "My name's Helen."

Man says pleasure. Helen shakes man's pinkie. Man laughs, moves to barstool between them.

"Look," says Helen. "I know you must hate people bothering you and I don't want to sound like just another football groupie but I know who you are."

Helen says man's name. Man ducks head, says you got it.

"I just had to make sure it was really you. My housemates will die. We watch you every week and we think you're terrific."

Man holds up casts. "I'm not so terrific now."

"Oh, but you will be again as soon as they heal. Really, I'm not just saying this, I think you have the best pair of hands in the league. I know I probably sound silly and infantile but really I've seen these hands make so many catches, *impossible* catches." She leans forward, touches his casts. "Really, these hands are magic."

"Thank you," man says. He pulls casts back as wife comes out of ladies room. She stands behind him, hand on hip.

"I see we've moved to a more comfortable spot," she says.

"I couldn't hear the game," man says. "That guy up there, he was getting really obnoxious."

Wife nods. "He wasn't before?"

"Oh," Helen says, "you didn't see. He was going to beat up his wife but your husband made him stop."

Wife looks at her. "My hero," wife says.

Man hooks foot in rung of empty barstool, pulls it out. "Sit down, honey," he says. "This is Helen."

"I'm delighted." Wife leans on man's shoulder. "What high school do you attend, Helen?"

Helen smiles. "I'm in college, third year at Case Western."

Man smiles. "What's your major?"

"Poly Sci."

"Really?" says man. "That's what I got *my* degree in."

"Imagine that," wife says. She squeezes man's shoulder. "Honey," she says. "Let's take a booth."

"I'm watching the game."

"You can watch it from the booth."

"Not good you can't." Man sees Helen turn away, look up at tube. Time out on field. "Come on," man says softly. "Just sit down and watch the game with me."

Wife's eyes glisten dark. "Just me, you, and another adoring fan."

"Somebody has to be."

Wife stands back: eyes glaze, face gets trembly hard look man's seen before.

"Don't even start," man says.

"I'm taking a booth," wife says. "You do what you want."

Wife sits in booth nearest door, back turned to rest of bar. Man sees Howard watching her over shoulder. Bartender looks at man, raises eyebrow, takes drink to man's wife. He leans over booth a while, listening. Man turns to game. Seattle punts. Helen clears throat.

"Your wife's very beautiful," she says.

"Thank you," says man.

"I hope I haven't caused any trouble."

Man stares at casts. "She gets a little jealous."

Helen says not on *her* account, she hopes. Man shrugs, says why not: Helen's young, she's friendly, she's pretty. That's enough. Helen asks does man really think she's pretty.

Man stares at her. She lowers eyes.

"I'll be honest," man says. "I don't want you to think I have any ulterior motive although I'd be lying if I said I have absolutely no interest but I'm sure you've heard a million times how refreshingly gorgeous you are. Mostly though I'm just enjoying talking to you. Okay?"

Helen says okay, she enjoys talking with man too, but maybe he'd better join wife. Man glances at wife's rigid back, says best to let her cool off. Helen sighs, says jealousy's such an awful thing, so debilitating. Man agrees one hundred percent. Stabler scores on pass to Burrough. They watch replay. Helen says she knows she promised but she's dying to know. How did man break hands? Man takes deep breath, says what the hell, it's really stupid. Man broke hands punching phone pole. Helen asks was man drunk. Man nods. Helen asks did it hurt a lot. Man nods. Helen wants to know whatever possessed man to punch phone pole of all things.

Man shrugs. "Couldn't reason with it."

Bartender brings another round. "Wife need anything?"

Man shakes head, looks over. "I'll check," he says. Man crosses room, squats down, rests casts on seat. "Need anything?" he says.

Wife stares into drink.

Man runs pinkie down wife's leg; she pushes cast away.

"Come on," man says. "Don't be like this."

Wife looks up, eyes wide and wet. "I don't believe you," she says. "I don't believe you keep doing what you're doing."

Man says keep doing what, what's he supposed to be doing, he's not doing anything. Wife clenches teeth, chokes, stiffarms man hard in chest: man rocks back, falls on ass. Wife stands, walks towards door. Man gets up, catches wife's arm with left cast. Wife snaps arm away. Man winces, catches wife in crook of arm, hugs tight.

"Please," man says, low and fast, "don't make a scene."

"You told her," wife says.

"Told her what? Told *who* what?"

"Let *go* of me," wife says, struggling. "You told her. You blamed it on me. Let me *go*."

"Mustn't touch a woman," says Howard from bar.

"Shut up," man says. "I didn't tell anybody anything. Just please don't get so excited."

Wife whips head back and forth, claws at casts. *"Let me go!"*

She's crying now. Man lets go.

"I'm sorry," he says. "I got nothing to be sorry about, but I'm sorry anyway. I don't know what to do."

"I don't give a fuck what you do," wife says, and she runs out door.

Man turns slowly. Eyes down bar look away.

"See?" says Howard. "They never lay off."

Man walks to end of bar, sits next to Helen, watches commercial on tube.

"Aren't you going to follow her?" says Helen.

"I'm watching the game," man says. "It's important."

"It's over," Helen says.

Man looks at her. Gentle blue eyes. Faint rash of freckles across bridge of nose he hadn't noticed before. Can't help noticing now.

"What was the score?" he says.

"35-17 Houston."

"Damn," says man. "You in a hurry to get anywhere?"

Helen says not really, home eventually, but she lives just around corner. Man says no kidding where. Man says what do you know, he lives right across street. Man says now that she mentions it, he *did* notice three girls moving in last month, but, you know, wife doesn't much like him noticing.

"We noticed you," Helen says. She lowers eyes. "You know."

Man orders drinks, says wife doesn't understand him, she's always jealous, they fight constantly, it's driving him crazy. Helen knows what man means. Man orders more drinks. Helen rests elbow on man's knee, says she's getting drunk. They laugh. Man orders one last round, says he's worried about hands. Will they heal right. Will they make impossible catches again. Helen strokes man's pinkies, says she's confident. Man strokes flannel with plaster, says he likes Helen. Helen says she likes man too but she's confused. She's never, well, you know, he's a married man. Man says he can talk to her, nothing to be confused about. Does Helen come here often. Helen says she'll probably come more often now. She giggles, downs drink. Man smiles.

Bartender comes over. What can he do for them. Helen looks at watch, says it's dark already, helps man dig wallet out of pants to settle tab.

Man leads way for door, Helen weaving in tow. Howard grins over shoulder, eyes Helen up and down, raises glass to man.

"Smooth move, champ," he slurs, winking.

Man stops, considers kicking Howard's stool out from under him, instead points long hard cast, furrows brow.

"I don't like you," man says.

"No kidding." Howard smiles, sips drink, swallows. "I'm your biggest fan."

"Oh, shut up," Helen says.

Howard says don't tell *him* shut up, but Helen and man are outside running down street, laughing, leaning on each other. They slow, walk. Man reaches; Helen clings to arm.

Streetlights arrow downtown to where Municipal Stadium squats on Lake Erie. Come winter, winds off lake cut cold and sharp across field; hands numb so bad ball feels like stainless steel bat out of hell. After game, hands thaw and throb, swell up soft, pink, useless. Man and Helen turn corner, walk slow, eyes down, talking. This winter man'll warm buns on bench. Next season could be playing for Houston, San Diego, Dallas even. Pack up, move on, start fresh.

Man stops two doors from home, points to telephone pole. "That's the one."

Helen grazes knuckles down pole, tilts head. "I just can't see you doing it."

Man scuffs shoe on sidewalk, glances up street. Light burns through bedroom window. Man says he's going to tell Helen something he's never told anybody, not even coach.

"Don't tell me if you don't want to," she says.

Man wants to, tells her how Thursday night he couldn't sleep worrying about Pittsburgh secondary. So he and wife went out to corner bar for nightcap. Wife sat talking to bartender; man felt edgy, walked around, ended up talking to woman sitting alone in booth. No big deal, no designs, just nice to talk to woman besides wife now and then. Wife came over, made scene, stormed out. Man followed, caught up right here, swung wife around, pinned her against phone pole. Wife cursed man. Man held wife tighter. Wife cursed man worse, fought, screamed, slapped man. Man threw wife down. Wife sprawled on ground crying, said man didn't love her. Man said he did. Wife called man fucking liar. Man got mad, felt like kicking wife's ass, told wife so. Wife said go ahead, you want to do it do it. Man froze, fists clenched. Wife said go ahead you shit fuck prick. Man turned to phone pole, squared off, punched left right left right methodical powerful body punches crunch crunch crunch crunch. Then man fell over.

"Oh, oh, oh," says Helen. She hugs casts to her.

Man walks Helen to her door. She reaches up, kisses man's cheek. Man kisses her cheek. She kisses man's lips. Man kisses her lips. She presses against man, pokes tongue in man's mouth. Man sucks, wraps casts around her.

"Do you want to come in?" Helen says.

"I don't think I better," man says. "I better get home." He looks at her. "Maybe some better time."

"Okay," says Helen. "I like you. I probably shouldn't, you're married and everything. But I do. A lot."

"I like you too," man says.

Crossing street man considers next step. Wife will have chain lock on door. Man will have to break it. Won't be first time. Once man's in, wife will come out of bedroom. She'll be dressed in man's orange and brown practice jersey she always sleeps in. Man's name and number will be on back. She'll stand solid, arms folded, face set. Man will throw heavy arms wide, try to talk, try to reason. But wife won't listen. Wife will curse man.

"Don't start," man will say.

Summer Rape Tally Hits Record High

Brenda and Manny have been lovers for the past four months. They met at work, started dating, and soon enough he was spending two or three nights a week at her place. Lately, Manny's been thinking about asking Brenda to move in with him. He loves her, he's sure of it, he's never met a woman of such strength and character combined with such grace and beauty before, and he's afraid for her: her neighborhood's not exactly the safest in the world. He wants to love her and protect her for a long, long time, he thinks, though he hasn't told her this yet.

He doesn't have to, as it turns out. Brenda can sense the change in him, and she's not sure she likes it. Manny's been a fun lover—considerate, boyish in an endearingly gentle way, lively in bed—but lately he's been getting pushy.

Brenda doesn't like being pushed.

So the more Manny asserts his protectiveness—holding his arm around her in line at the movies, butting in on conversations she's having with other men at work, cautioning her on how to dice onions in the kitchen—the more Brenda asserts her independence—pulling her hand from his and dancing through traffic between crosswalks, shyly flirting back with her middle-aged boss at work who she knows is harmless, running her daily five miles in the park across the street after sunset.

"Come on," Manny tells her one night in bed after they've made love. "I'm not trying to restrict your freedom; reality restricts everybody's freedom. I'm just saying a woman's got to be careful, that's all. Jesus," he says. "Don't jump all over me." He rolls away from her, crosses his arms in a tight-lipped sulk.

Brenda moves next to him, runs fingers through his dark, curly hair. "I'm sorry," she says. "But I told you, I'm careful."

"Running alone in the park after dark is careful?"

"It's too hot before sunset."

"So run in the morning."

"I can barely get to work on time as is."

"So don't run."

Brenda slaps her belly. "I'll get fat."

"Fat chance." He strokes her narrow hips. "You're all muscle, lean and mean."

Brenda smiles. "It's not for the exercise, really," she says. "I just like to run."

"What's to like? Racquetball's a lot more fun. I could teach you. We could play together. Running's so boring. You just run and run until it hurts to run anymore. How much sense does that make?"

Brenda's heard this before. People who don't run just can't understand. Sure, it hurts to run. When she started running five years ago, she thought she'd die after the first quarter-mile: lungs burned, head throbbed, stomach cramped, calves knotted up—she was a mess. But the trick, she found out, is to just keep running, keep moving, keep going forward until you outrun the pain. Oh, the pain's still there, sure, you never really leave the pain behind, but when you're really running you're staying a step ahead of the pain, and you're focusing on a spot that's always a step ahead of you where you can see yourself running. You look so good there running in front of yourself. You look whole and perfect. You've hit your true stride now, and now you're racing yourself to a final-kick photo-finish dead-heat draw and you just can't beat yourself.

The feeling's wonderful.

But how can Brenda explain it all to Manny? He's not a runner. "I just like to run," she says again. "And I like to run at night."

"I'm talking to a wall." Manny lights a cigarette, blows smoke through clenched teeth. "Didn't you read the paper this morning?"

"I read it."

"There's a goddamn epidemic out there. This town's lousy with creeps and perverts and psychos and just plain horny high school jerk-offs with their balls boiling over, and I think half of them hang out in the bushes waiting to watch you run by."

"Don't exaggerate."

"Wait a minute," he says, jumping out of bed. He pulls on a pair of cutoffs. "Just hang on." He leaves the room, comes back with the city section from this morning's newspaper, drops it in her lap. The headline screams at her; his finger stabs mid-article. "Recognize the name of this park? There've been three rapes there this month alone."

"I read it," Brenda says. She tosses the paper to the floor, glares up at Manny. "One of those was during the day. Another one the woman was with her boyfriend who has a brown belt in some kind of karate. The rapist held him at gunpoint, had the woman tie him to a tree with his own belt, and made him watch. So how careful can you be? What do you want me to do? Hide in my apartment twenty-four hours a day, get a sex change operation, what?"

"Join a spa, run with friends, I don't care!" Manny paces, runs both hands from forehead to crown, shakes his head. "What the hell's the big deal? Make me happy one time. Just stay out of the goddamn park for awhile."

"Why don't you just leave," she tells him. "I don't feel like company anymore tonight."

Manny's eyes moisten. He stares at the ceiling, bites his lip, nods, turns for the door, stops, turns around again.

"You can really hurt me sometimes, you know," he says, voice husky.

"I know," Brenda says. "I don't mean to."

He sits on the edge of the bed, touches her hand. "All I'm saying is I worry about you. Try to understand."

"I understand," Brenda says. "I understand, I understand, I understand." She grips his arm, takes a deep breath. "Now you try to understand. I've lived here for seven years. I've been running in that park for five years. This is my neighborhood. That's my park. That's where I go to hear the birds and smell the trees and feel the breeze in my face and be alone with myself and no, don't even say it, it's not the same being alone in my apartment behind a row of deadlocks."

"Okay," Manny says. "Take it easy, I know what you're saying, and I'm just going to say one more thing and then I'll shut up. Birds and trees and bees, wonderful, but women are getting raped out there, and I wish you'd be more careful. That's all. Just stop and think. Imagine how you'd feel if you were raped."

But Brenda doesn't have to imagine. Six years ago, she was raped in this very same apartment. She hasn't told anybody about it since she told the women in her first session with the rape counseling group, and everybody else told their stories, each one more horrible than the one before, it seemed, until finally a pale, hollow-eyed mother of three told of the man who had followed her to her car from the mall one evening and held a butcher knife to her six month old's throat and said give me what I want or I hand you her head, and Brenda ran out in tears never to return.

So she's never told Manny how in the middle of the night one night, a man in a ski mask jimmied the lock and woke her in this very same bed with a gun to her head. "I've seen you around," he said in a high, grunting voice that sounded fake. "Don't scream, don't fight." "I won't," she said, "please, be careful." "I've seen you around. Don't look at me. Look at me and I have to kill you." She closed her eyes. "I can't see you," she said, "I don't know you." "Oh, you know me, baby," he said, voice shaking, "you just don't know who I am. Relax, now, easy, easy," and she held her breath and felt him pulling her nightgown off and felt his weight pinning her and straining at her and she let out her breath and held it again and heard him cursing. He slapped her then. Then again and again. "Wait a minute," he said. "Move and I kill you."

He got off her and she heard him in the living room knocking things over. She opened her eyes and thought now, now, run, run, run, get out of here! but she couldn't move, and she found herself praying he wouldn't come back, maybe if she just lay there and closed her eyes and prayed hard enough he wouldn't come back, he'd just leave, but then she heard him and opened her eyes and he was back carrying an extension cord. He tied her wrists together and dragged her to the floor and made her face away from him. "That's better," he said.

He raped her three times that night, dragging her from room to room looking for different things to tie her to, and then he left.

Her description of her assailant was, the police said, "inadequate."

She thought of moving, but her apartment was rent-controlled, and the police had assured her that rapists rarely victimize the same victim again. Instead, she had iron bars installed on her windows, a row of deadbolts on her door. For the next year she hurried home from work each day and locked herself in, heart thumping every time the furnace kicked on or footsteps echoed up the stairway.

Then one evening around dusk, a pigeon whirred and flapped on her windowsill, and Brenda jumped up and started running. Down the stairs, across the street, into the park she ran and ran until she couldn't run anymore. The next day she bought sweatshirt, sweatpants, and running shoes.

So now she runs, every night, and every night the rape struggles to keep up with her. It's still there. She's managed to put some distance on it, so that to recall it now is almost like reading about it in the newspaper, but how can any woman reading of a rape deny that it's happened to her as well? It's there, lagging behind her as she picks up her pace. She runs.

"I know how you feel," Manny's saying. "Rape's the kind of thing that happens to somebody else, never to you, right? Wrong. It happens. And all I'm saying is that maybe you can't avoid all the crazies and psychos in the world, but you sure as hell don't have to advertise yourself to them, which is what you're doing in that park every night whether you know it or not. You're just asking for trouble."

"Shut up," Brenda says.

Manny grips her shoulders. "No, for once you shut up. You wouldn't walk into a bikers bar in high heels, miniskirt, and fishnet stockings, would you?"

"It's not the same. Let go."

"I've seen you running out there. I've seen the way you look. And I've seen the way some of those bums look at you when you pass by. I know what they're thinking." Manny's grip tightens, eyes flash like a jolt of voltage. "I'm scared for you," he says.

Brenda stares at him, eyes widening. "No," she says softly. "No more."

She pulls away from him, goes to the closet, pulls on her grey jogging suit.

"Brenda, come on."

She sits next to him on the bed and laces her sneakers.

"Brenda, please, give me a break, huh?" He touches her shoulder, her hair. "You don't have to prove a point."

"This has nothing to do with you," she says. She kisses him quickly and trots to the door, throws the locks and chains, and she's running, running out of the building, across the street, and into the night. She glances over her shoulder and Manny is huffing and puffing barefooted far behind her, calling her name again and again, telling her that it's after midnight for godsakes, please, please come back, but she's already cutting past the hedges and through the trees and his voice grows faint against the regular rhythm of breathing in her ears, a pulse she can feel working its way from her head to her lungs to her heart, down her belly and spreading warm across her hips and thighs as her knees pull high, legs drive down, and feet hit the soft grass for only an instant. A breeze lifts from the trees and she paces it, head thrown back, stars cutting through the city's summer haze bright and cold for her eyes only.

There's danger in the park, yes, she knows, she doesn't need the newspaper or Manny to tell her that. Brenda can feel it all around her, behind every bush she passes, behind every tree, just outside the circle of light cast by the lamppost up ahead, trailing her every step. But she's running now, moving cleanly and smoothly, running much too fast for anything to catch up.

Election Year

It came to him while he was watching TV one night. Lauren had taken the kids to bed and—a half-hour gone now—had probably gone to sleep herself, leaving Al up alone again, drinking beers and staring down the picture tube.

A commercial came on: a long-legged model wrapped in a towel stepped out of a sunken circular bath, began splashing cologne all over herself. The camera followed the towel dropping in slow-motion folds to her feet; picture dissolved to close shots of shimmering legs, arms, back: she splashed cologne on her throat, neck arched back in profile, mouth opening, eyes closed. Cologne cascaded dreamlike down out of sight between her breasts. She dabbed some behind an ear. Long red nails trailed wetly up a calf to the crook of her knee, leg stretched taut and smooth, toes pointing heavenward.

"Woof," Al said.

Then a tight shot of her mesmerized face—moist red lips curling apart, head ducking slightly, impossibly dark eyes slowly rising—while a breathlessly coy female voiceover crooned the name of the cologne and its slogan: *For the Experience.*

"God in heaven," Al told the TV. "Uh, uh, uh."

He wondered briefly if the stuff smelled any good, whether Lauren would like a bottle—her birthday was coming up end of the month—and then in one of those rare and wonderful moments of clarity that sometimes hit us late at night and make what we do appear suddenly significant, Al Muzhikovsky understood how wrong he'd been.

A paid political announcement came on: the incumbent presidential candidate asked Al if he were better off now than he was four years ago. Al wondered. He pictured the cologne model, felt the familiar flutter of his heart, knew he wanted her. And that was stupid. She was videotape.

He wandered into the kitchen for another beer, walked back out without it, finally went outside and stared past Arlington's glowing sky towards a blur of foggy stars. He kicked through soggy leaves he'd meant to rake last weekend.

Then he decided.

Back inside he checked on Nicholas and Lisa, kissed each smooth and innocent forehead, filled his heart until his throat ached. Then he left them and lay down beside Lauren. He snuggled up against her, kissed her ear. She stirred, shifted, flung a warm leg over his.

This was his wife. He'd married her nine years ago. She'd mothered two fine children he was crazy about. He knew he loved her, but over the years the day-to-day ebb and flow of domestic trivia had somehow numbed the feeling. Al decided now to love her and hold her and keep her and cling to her and to no other all the days of his life.

He'd have to break the news to Wendi tomorrow.

Once a week, twice a week tops, Al Muzhikovsky spent an hour, two hours, three hours tops making love with Wendi Trussel, and so far as he could tell, Lauren remained unsuspecting. This had been going on for nearly a year now. Wendi waited tables, lunch and dinner, at Mr. Claude's USA cafe in Georgetown, where Al was manager in charge of purchasing.

The next day, as usual, Al was up before dawn and off to the markets to order the daily fare of fresh fish, meats, and produce. He finished by nine o'clock, sat in his office above the restaurant staring out the window at M Street below. A white-aproned Cuban boy across the street was hosing down the sidewalk in front of a Vietnamese restaurant. Today was Thursday, Wendi's day off. Usually he found time in the afternoon to stroll up to her English basement efficiency on Q Street. Sometimes he bought flowers from a street vendor along the way.

Not today, though.

Instead, he rehearsed what he had to say, picked up the phone, called her, told her it was over. She sounded sleepy, confused. *What* was over?

"Us," Al said.

He heard rustling sounds, Wendi saying hold it, wait a minute. He pictured her muffling the phone in her pillow, sitting up in bed, rubbing her eyes.

"Now," she said. "What?"

"I can't see you again," Al said. "I mean, alone, privately. I can see you at work, but I can't see you at your place."

"Why not?"

Al took a deep breath, explained his decision of last night: he loved his wife, he loved his kids, he wouldn't hurt them for the world, it just wasn't fair to them. Blah, blah, blah: he hated the stuffy sound of his voice as he reminded her of what they'd agreed to from the start, that he'd never leave his wife and kids, that she couldn't live with the thought of breaking up a marriage, that theirs was a day-to-day affair—special, exciting, ultimately crazy. No promises, no regrets.

"I feel good about this past year," Al said, "but I feel relieved that it's over. How about you?"

Wendi didn't answer.

"I'm sorry," Al said. "Don't cry. Please."

"Just tell me why all of a sudden."

"I just told you."

"You told me shit. Why now? Why not six months ago? Why not six months from now?"

Al didn't know. The boy across the street was polishing the restaurant's brass door handles. Light flashed from out of his hand.

"Why now?" she said again, voice breaking.

Al started, stopped. "Lauren knows," he said finally, and felt instantly foolish.

"God," Wendi said. "How?"

Al closed his eyes. "I told her."

"Why?"

"I had to. I can't lie to her anymore."

"Oh," Wendi said. "Oh. God, how did she take it?"

"She was hurt. She got mad."

"What did she say?"

"She said a lot of things." Al tried to imagine how Lauren would react. His face burned; he switched the receiver to his other ear. "No," he said. "I never told her. I wouldn't do that. She doesn't know."

"She doesn't."

"No."

"Why did you tell me she did?"

"I guess I thought it would be easier. I don't know."

Wendi laughed suddenly. Al laughed with her, he felt so stupid, but Wendi went on laughing some time after Al stopped.

"It's not supposed to be easy," she said, finally. Her voice trembled. "I can't believe you're doing this over the phone. You can't face me? That's chickenshit bullshit."

She was right, of course, so Al agreed to meet her as soon as he could get away.

"Now," Wendi said. "I'll come there."

No good, Al told her. All right then, Wendi said, come to her place. Al pictured the unmade pull-out sofa, babydoll cotton underthings draped across the arms. Again, no good. He had a few things to take care of first, liquor inventory and so forth, then he'd come pick her up. They'd drive somewhere.

"Anywhere you want," Al said.

"You're the boss," Wendi said. "It's up to you."

Al's assistants, Saffa and Kevin, were receiving a delivery of meats through the metal doors in the sidewalk when Al got to the basement. Kevin dragged a metal basket of plastic-bagged hamburger towards the prep kitchen just past the walk-in coolers. "What kind of choice is that?" he called behind him. He looked up. "Hey, Al."

Saffa backed another laden basket down the metal slide. "It is the only choice you have," he said. He swung the basket to the floor, muscles bunching and loosening in a clean, easy flow.

Al unlocked the liquor cage, fixed an inventory sheet to his clipboard.

Kevin returned from the kitchen, white apron hanging bloody and untied at the waist. "You catch the debates last night, Al?" He reached behind him, fumbled with the loose strings. "What shit. Election year, they promise you anything."

Saffa appeared at the door of the cage, tied the apron for Kevin. "Still," he said, "though the decision must cause each voter much turmoil, a choice must be made."

Kevin winced. "That's pushing it, Saf." He grinned at Al. "Saffa's word for the day." Al smiled, started counting bottles, the soft drone of his workers playing like Muzak in the background. Saffa had worked for him three years now. He was from Botswana in South Africa, attended night classes at George Washington University on a student visa. Short, heavily muscled, dark-skinned and darker-eyed, Saffa spoke gravely and carefully on all matters, from politics to being shorted on a delivery. He was staunchly but dispassionately pro-American, hoped one day to become a citizen. Al had only seen him flare up once: a Sudanese busboy had criticized U.S. ties with Israel. "Go back to the fucking Sudan, boy," Saffa screamed at him, spittle flying. "Man, you eat garbage, boy, you eat the shit of a pig!" Two cooks held back the busboy to keep Saffa from hurting him.

Al had hired Kevin to help Saffa six months ago. He was white—the only white in a basement of blacks and hispanics—and unknown to most of his fellow workers held a Master's degree in English literature. "Why do you want a shit job like this?" Al had asked him. Kevin had answered evenly: he had to eat, he had to pay rent, it was steady work, jobs in English lit weren't easy to come by. "Figure I'll go on for the Ph.D. one of these days," he said, "but not right now, I'm so sick of school. I'll give you a good year at least, that's a promise."

You couldn't hope for much more in the restaurant trade.

As it turned out, Kevin and Saffa made a good team. They worked silently at first, but soon enough they were lost in conversation as they hefted and toted side-by-side. Wendi often visited them on breaks.

"Quit flirting with my men," Al told her once, only half joking.

Her eyes danced. "Gotta keep in practice."

She called them the Twins, told Al how Saffa had begun to open up, how he'd asked Kevin to help him with his accent, how Kevin had bought Saffa a copy of *Word Power*, a word-per-day vocabulary builder, how Saffa was teaching Kevin Setswana, a language, she said, which was as exuberant and lyrical as Saffa's English was solemn and serious.

"They're so cute together," Wendi told him one Thursday

afternoon in bed, "like they should be dressed in those little red jackets and holding lanterns on either side of your driveway."

"Jesus," Al had said. "I'm having an affair with a racist."

"Equal opportunity racist," Wendi said, and she'd trailed her fingers up the back of his neck.

Al's heart quickened thinking of her.

His problem, he realized now as he worked his way from the Cutty to the Chivas, probably stemmed from his inexperience with women. All through high school and college he'd been shy, stumblingly awkward, acne-afflicted. Dates had been few and routinely uncomfortable. Sex had been desperately plain: the occasional uninspiring coed who he considered even homlier than he granting him unexpected and undeserved favor in return for an otherwise uneventful evening. Then a couple of years after college, things began to change. He was promoted from assistant floor manager to purchasing agent at Mr. Claude's, a job that included buying for the two other Mr. Claude's in Virginia and Maryland. Local sales reps began taking him to lunch, dinner, parties. He joined a health club, swam, lifted, played racquetball twice a week: his once gawky frame began to move more purposefully. He kept his hair trimmed short, shaved his scraggly beard: his face took on a rough, angular sort of interestingness. He'd read in the paper that Washington D.C. offered five eligible females for each eligible male: he began to believe this.

Suddenly, he was meeting women, both on and off the job, and these women were looking at him in a way he'd never seen women look at him before. They smiled, cast their eyes sideways at him in elevators; they invited him for drinks, for dinner, and they asked him questions about his life and work and opinions and listened when he answered as though his answers mattered very much indeed.

Al had developed poise. His big, nervous, goofy post-adolescent grin had somehow metamorphosed into an amazingly charming and disarming boyish smile. Or so intimated a secretary for a D.C. produce wholesaler, who stared distractedly at him over her snifter of Gran Marnier one evening and cupped his hand with hers when he held a match for her cigarette. Her name was Lauren. She was tall, had large breasts, boyish hips, skinny legs. She sat erect, shoulders back, chin high as she blew smoke towards the ceiling. She looked good dressed in blue.

Her knee had grazed against his beneath the table. Again and again.

"That smile of yours looks *so* innocent," she'd said.

Al blushed, smiled more. "It is," he said. "It really is."

Eight months later they were married. Two years later Nicholas was born, and Lauren gave up her job. Lisa came two years after that. Then, when Lisa was four years old, Al stayed for a drink at Mr. Claude's after work and saw a new waitress with a tray full of cocktails negotiating her way through the happy-hour crush. She was short, plumpish, baby-faced. A blonde wisp fell from her bunned hair, trailed across a dimpled cheek. The bartender told Al her name was Wendi.

"Cute," the bartender said, "but what is she, sixteen?"

The next time she came to the bar for drinks, Al introduced himself.

The following evening, he stayed for a drink again. And another drink. And another. He found something to say to her each time she came to the bar. He liked the way her nose flared when she laughed. He made her laugh again and again. After the dinner rush, Wendi checked out, joined him. They talked, they laughed, Wendi touched his arm, Al leaned towards her. Wendi told Al she was twenty-three, just out of college, making some money until she figured out what she wanted to do. Al told Wendi she reminded him of a certain model on a California beach in a Coca-Cola commercial. Wendi told Al he was cute. Al called Lauren, said he was drinking with friends, wouldn't be home for awhile. Lauren told Al please take a cab if you can't drive. Two hours and several drinks later, Al and Wendi were making love on the floor of his office upstairs.

Afterward, Wendi told Al she felt just awful, he was married, had kids, she wasn't the homewrecker type, but she hadn't been able to stop. Al held her, said it was a first for him too. What was done was done, they agreed, but they wouldn't do it again. Then next week they made love again, but they swore that was it. Then three days later they made love again.

"Is this just infatuation?" Wendi said.

Al thought hard. "I think so."

"Not love?"

"I don't think so," Al said. "What do you think?"

Wendi moved her hand from his chest. "I don't think it's love," she said quietly, "but whatever it is, it's hard to stop."

"Maybe we shouldn't stop," Al had said. "Not right now, anyway."

Al was having a difficult time keeping his mind on the inventory. Saffa and Kevin had finished with the delivery and, perched on a stack of liquor boxes outside the cage, were taking a break. Saffa was reading aloud from an editorial in the *Post*, his voice low, melodic, mesmerizing.

"What shit," Kevin interrupted.

Al lost count again on the Dubonnet. "Hey," he said. "You guys got some work to do?"

Kevin grinned. "We work when we work, man. Don't get all bossy on us." He hooked his fingers through the wire mesh, leaned against the cage. "So who are you voting for, Al?" he said. "You a Democrat like everybody else in this town?"

"Haven't given it much thought."

"Typical voter. You know what?" Kevin said. "I'm not even going to vote this time around. I mean, did you *see* those debates? This is a no-win election."

"Guess so," Al said.

"But you must make a choice," Saffa said. He stood, put a hand on Kevin's shoulder. "This is your privileged duty."

Kevin shrugged. "Can't choose when there's nothing to choose *between.*"

"If I had the right to vote, I would make the choice. I would choose," Saffa said carefully, "to the best of my knowledge," he went on, "the best man for the job."

"Perfect," Kevin said. He shook his head, laughed. "Tell you what. You tell me who you want to vote for, I'll vote for him for you."

Saffa looked from Kevin to Al, frowned. "No man can cast another man's vote."

"Who says? Hey, Al, the man wants to vote, he ain't got a vote. I got a vote, I don't want to vote. Makes sense, huh?"

Al slapped the clipboard down on the shelf in front of him. A bottle rolled, exploded on the floor.

"Hey," Al said. "I have things to do. You guys want to work? Finish this inventory for me."

They stared at him. "Okay, boss," Saffa said.

Al brushed past them, headed for the stairs, face hot, hands trembling.

"What's wrong with him?" he heard Kevin whisper.

"Turmoil," Saffa answered.

Al drove up to Wendi's house, double-parked in front, saw her sitting on the stoop of the upstairs apartment, head down. Up the block, pre-schoolers shouted and squealed, raced their Big Wheels and tricycles down the cobblestone sidewalk. They made Al feel fatherly. He got out, called to her. Wendi raised her head, stared blankly, slowly stood. She was dressed in her waitressing uniform: black trousers, black bow tie hanging untied from the open collar of her white ruffled shirt, white sneakers. Her pony tail bobbed.

She got in, buckled up, folded her arms across her chest. Her eyes glared dull and red.

"Why the uniform?" Al said.

"Sharon called in. I have to take her shift this afternoon. In an hour."

"I'll get you there. Anywhere special you want to go now?"

Wendi stared straight ahead, silent.

Al drove down the block, took Wisconsin to M street, turned off at Pennsylvania and headed towards the Capitol. He figured they could take a walk through the Mall, maybe. There was time for that. They passed the White House. Important things going on in there, Al knew. Decisions that affected the world. He'd really have to figure out how he was voting.

"I'm sorry," he said, finally.

Wendi looked at him. "Listen," she said, voice low and shaking, "after you called me today, I felt like shit. I didn't know what to do. I called my mother." She laughed; her voice caught. "I haven't told my mother anything about my life since I was fourteen, but this morning I told her all about you and me and asked her what I should do. She asked me if I loved you."

"Wendi," Al said.

"Just let things go on with us for awhile."

Al watched her lower lip tremble a moment. "I can't," he said.

"God," Wendi said, and she began to cry. Al pulled over, put a hand on her shoulder. She stiffened. "My mother told me that if I loved you, I shouldn't give you up. She said the hell with his wife, who cares if she'll be hurt, better her than you. She said you sound like the kind of guy who'll get tired of his wife again sooner or later only next time it'll be with someone else, somebody who'll get you to leave her."

"Your mother doesn't know me."

"She asked if you loved me. I said I think so, but you just felt too guilty to admit it, and don't tell me you don't love me because I can't take hearing that right now."

Al hadn't planned on telling her he didn't love her. After all, he'd never actually told her he *did* love her.

"Wendi," he said again.

"Don't talk," she said. "Listen. This is what I want. I want us to stay lovers. That or I'm going to call your wife and tell her what we've been doing."

Al stared at her. He opened his mouth, but he didn't know what to say.

"I mean it," she said.

He started the car, pulled onto the street, turned around, headed back towards Georgetown.

"I mean it, Al. I'm not asking you to leave her and the kids. That was what my mother told me to do. I'm just saying keep the status quo."

They were passing the White House again. Al slowed down, stared at it. "Who're you voting for?" he said.

Wendi took her hand from her eyes. "Don't make me laugh."

Back at Mr. Claude's, Al stayed in his office as much as possible, but once, on the way to the kitchen, he saw Wendi taking a customer's order. She looked at him, wide eyes clouding, and he quickly looked away. Saffa called him to the basement once to check on a delivery of romaine lettuce. He wrenched a slat off a crate, pulled out a head speckled brown near the stalk.

"Freezer burn," Saffa said.

"It's not too bad," Al said.

Kevin shook his head, eyed Al oddly as he left.

On the drive home to Arlington, Al had a chance to think. Wendi wouldn't tell Lauren, he decided. That would be an evil thing to do, and Wendi wasn't evil. In fact, she was a sensitive, good-hearted, generous person.

But what if she *did* tell?

While Lauren fixed dinner, Al tumbled and wrestled with

Nicholas and Lisa. He tickled Lisa so much that she broke into tears, kept crying until Lauren picked her up.

"I'm sorry," he said.

Lauren stroked Lisa's back. "That's okay. Just don't overdo it."

"Lisa's a big baby," Nicholas cried, tugging at Al's leg.

During dinner, Al talked about work, and Lauren listened attentively, asked the right questions, nodded in the right places, offered helpful comments and opinions. He relied on her. She was steady, intelligent, sensible, and she listened so well and understood what he was talking about so completely that he took her for granted. Suddenly he wanted her to talk. He wanted to listen to her, understand her. But he didn't know quite how to start.

After dinner, Al helped Lauren clear the table, something he liked to think he did regularly but, he realized, something he did rarely at best. While he was wiping off the counter, the phone rang. Al paused, went on wiping. Lauren answered, listened, asked who was calling please, listened some more, held out the phone, eyebrows raised.

"Wendi somebody," she said.

Al took the phone.

"I'm sorry," Wendi said, "I shouldn't be calling you at home, I was going to tell you tomorrow at work but I thought maybe I better tell you tonight before you do something noble and stupid like tell Lauren yourself before she hears it from me. You didn't tell her anything, did you?"

"No," Al said.

"I didn't think you would. I thought you *might*, but I was pretty sure you wouldn't. I'm not going to tell her anything, Al. I couldn't do that. If it's over for us it's over. Does it really *have* to be over?"

"Yes."

Lauren touched his arm, moved him out of the way of the dishwasher.

"Okay," Wendi said. "I'll accept that. But I just want you to know, no one's ever hurt me the way you're hurting me right now."

Al rubbed his eyes, heard a deep moan in the background. "Who's there?" he said.

"Kevin. Your man Kevin." She giggled. "Our man Kevin. He just told me I'm being melodramatic. He's right. But I'm drunk so so what."

"What's he doing there?" Al said. Lauren glanced at him, went back to loading the dishwasher.

"He's been comforting me. He found me crying in the basement today. It was the only place to cry without a bunch of people staring at you. He walked me home after work. We bought a jug of Chablis, also a comfort. He's the one who told me what an awful thing it would be telling your wife. I think he's going to comfort me some more once I get off the phone. Are you jealous?"

"Yes," Al said. "But it doesn't make much difference."

"Are you talking in short noncommittal sentences so your wife won't suspect you're talking to your former lover?"

"Yes."

Wendi was silent a moment. "Then I'll let you go," she said, finally. "Bye."

Al hung up. Lauren looked up from rinsing a plate.

"Somebody from work," Al said.

Lauren's lips tightened. "You weren't very friendly."

She knew. Al was sure. Lauren knew. How long she'd known or how much she knew, he wasn't sure. But she knew. Al couldn't understand. How could she go on living with him, caring for him, making love to him, knowing all the while that he was making love with another woman? How could she laugh at his jokes? How could she tell the kids kiss your father, it's time for bed, knowing what he now knew she had to know? That he'd done things with another woman that he was only supposed to do with her. That he'd bared secrets to another woman, whispered sweetnesses to another woman, cried out passions to another woman that belonged to her, to Lauren, to *her*. How could she know all this and pretend not to? Al was afraid of the answer.

He sat on the couch with Lauren watching TV. He held her hand, and she let him. He turned to her, saw her profile lit by the flashing glow of a car chase scene. He'd done the right thing—it was over with Wendi, no return—and Wendi had been right, too—it wasn't supposed to be easy. But now he understood that doing the right thing *was* the easy part, and the hard part remained to be done.

A health spa commercial came on, and a woman in leg warmers and leotard danced across the screen.

Lauren squinted. "Do you think she's pretty?" she said.

"She's a model. She's supposed to be."

"Tough job," she said, "but somebody's got to do it."

Al squeezed her hand, waited for her to squeeze back, squeezed again. He pictured Wendi drinking wine and giggling with Kevin, rubbed his eyes until sparks flashed.

"Hey," he said, suddenly. "I meant to ask you, who are you voting for?"

Lauren looked at him, eyes glistening. "What brought that up?"

"I don't know, I was just thinking. First Tuesday of November's coming up quick and I don't even know who you're voting for."

Lauren lifted her chin, sat stiffly. "What difference does it make?"

"Come on," Al said. "I don't know who to vote for." He pulled her to him, kissed her neck. "Come on," he whispered. "Really. I'm your husband. You can tell me. I'm listening." He hugged her close, heard her breath turn ragged, felt his own arms trembling in the awkward embrace.

"Please," he said. "Just tell me."

No Visitors

Friday morning my father gets admitted to the hospital with a broken leg. Saturday afternoon my father's neighbor Gloria Isaacs calls and blames the whole thing on me: if I was the kind of son who took the time to drive forty minutes back to the old neighborhood to see his lonely old dad and maybe help out with the yardwork, then maybe he wouldn't have to climb up a shaky old ladder to clean the gutters all by himself.

"They operated last night," she says. "A rod and two screws, but thank God the hip's okay. I called him this morning and he told me not to tell you. Donald Reilly, I said, you old fool, your only son and nobody notified him yet? He said yeah, and let's keep it that way, Gloria." She takes a breath. "So you didn't hear it from me."

"How is he?"

"He sounds okay, but you know that hospital food. I can't get out to see him or else I would. My arthritis. Every joint in my body is on fire."

My wife won't go with me. Donny has a cub scout meeting this afternoon, she says, and she has to drive him there.

"Call a cab for him," I tell her.

"I'm not putting an eight year old in a cab by himself."

"So let him miss the meeting. He can come with us. What's more important?"

Kathy shakes her head. "I'm not taking him to the hospital. Donny hates hospitals. The smell makes him gag." She holds up her hand to stop me. "And if you want to know the absolute truth, which I know you know already, I don't like your father, and I don't much feel like visiting him and listening to him bitch and moan and get all nasty like he always does." She touches my cheek. "I'm sorry, but I just can't talk to that man."

"Neither can I. That's not the point. He's hurt, he needs us."

Kathy ducks her head. "I hate to say this, Michael, but he's your father. You're the one he needs."

So I drive down to see him myself.

I haven't been in Municipal Hospital since my mother died. That was ten years ago, the year before Kathy and I were married. Kathy came with me to the Oncology ward once, but Mom was too drugged to know it, and my father sat stone-faced and silent, holding Mom's hand, until we left. Afterwards he asked me not to bring Kathy again. It was a strain on my mother, he said, having strangers in the room.

"Kathy's not a stranger," I said.

He stared at me, eyes blinking hollowly. "This is a family thing," he said. "She's not family."

The hospital reeks of disinfectant and stale air conditioning. At the reception desk, a plump young nurse behind an IBM terminal tells me my father's allowed no visitors. I ask her what she means no visitors. She looks up from her screen, smiles brightly. "No one's allowed to see him," she says. "Mr. Reilly specifically requested."

"But I'm his son."

She types, studies the screen. "No exceptions. The patient

specifically requested." She smiles rosebuds and sugar. "Sorry, sir."

She can't be more than twenty-two, looks sixteen, all dimpled determination, professionally pleasant. Country girl, I imagine: big happy family full of wholesome brothers and sisters who tease her good-naturedly when she stays out on a date past midnight with her sweet gawky boyfriend who's going to marry her soon as he graduates from State University with his degree in Agricultural Engineering so he can pitch in and help out his father-in-law on the farm. I don't like to bully her, but I have no choice.

"Let me see your supervisor."

She keeps smiling. "You're looking at her."

"You're the supervisor?"

She nods. "We had a cutback, so they asked me to supervise myself. Is there a problem, sir?"

"Yes, there's a problem. I want to see my father, and the prissy little bureaucrat in charge of visiting won't let me."

Her eyes narrow. "Watch yourself, asshole," she says. "I'm working a double shift. I don't need this shit."

"I have a right to see my own father."

"Not when your own father doesn't want to see you." She looks me up and down. "And I can't say I blame him, sir, if this is the way you normally act."

My jaw tightens; I stare her hard in the eyes. "Listen to me, young lady," I say, low and icy, "as my father's only next of kin, I have certain legal obligations and privileges in a case such as this. If you deny me access to my father, this hospital could be liable for damages in a major law suit." I smile coolly. "I happen to be an attorney."

She smiles back. "Lawyers don't scare us," she says. "We're insured."

"I hate hospitals," I say. "They make me sick."

"Then leave. You'll feel better."

I leave.

I call Kathy from a phone booth across the street. "I'm not surprised," she says. "Your father is the most childish, stubbornest, nastiest man I've ever met. I'm sorry, Michael, but it's true. You know it's true."

"It hasn't always been true," I say.

"Long enough. Come home."

"He's my father, for godsakes. I can't just leave."

"What else can you do?"

I call Gloria Isaacs.

"Now you know what it feels like," she says. "Every evening I watch him sit on his front porch waiting for you to maybe pay him a little visit in his old age."

"All we do is fight, Gloria."

"Fighting's better than lonely, believe me. Me and Lenny, we have him over for dinner once a week. Afternoons I go over and sit and maybe play a little canasta, which he says he lives for. All he talks about is how he doesn't have a family since your mother died, how he never sees you anymore."

"It goes both ways," I say, feeling suddenly guilty. "I don't see him knocking at my door either."

"A son should visit his father."

"I keep in touch. I call him now and then."

"Calling is not seeing."

"I want to see him, Gloria."

"So see him."

"He won't let me."

"So call him."

She gives me his number. "He's in a semi-private with this rude Polish man. You'd think a person who's slaved his life away providing for his family would have a son who'd pay for a private room so he could suffer in peace."

I call.

"Kopanski," an efficient voice answers. "Who's this?"

"Michael Reilly," I say. "I'd like to speak to my father."

"Is that right. I've heard a lot about you, Michael. You're the ungrateful, unloving, know-it-all punk kid who's been driving your old man into an early grave."

"Hey, wait a minute."

"More or less his words, not mine. Listen, let me save you some time. First of all, he won't talk to you. Second, even if he wanted to talk to you, he couldn't. He can't get out of bed, the phone's on my side of the room, I'm laid up with a broken butt, I can't reach the phone to him, and if you think I can buzz a nurse to do it, you haven't spent much time in a hospital. Bye," he says, and he hangs up.

I call back.

"Kopanski," Kopanski answers. "Who's this?"

"I have to talk to him," I say.

"Impossible, kid, I told you."

"Gloria Isaacs talked to him."

"Dizzy old broad with a voice like a dentist's drill?"

"That's her."

"She didn't exactly talk to him. She talked to me. She said tell Donald I hope he's feeling better, so I told him. He said tell Gloria I'll live if the food don't kill me, so I told her. She said tell Donald he should know better than to be climbing ladders at his age, so I told him. He says tell Gloria maybe if I had a son who'd do it for me I wouldn't have to but I don't so I did, so I told her. She says tell Donald blah, blah, blah. I finally told your old man she said goodbye even when she didn't, I got so sick of the conversation."

"Could you please just ask my father why he won't let me see him?"

"What am I, his answering service? I'm a busy man, kid. I got a million people calling me every five minutes asking for decisions that are vital to the operation of my business. I run a consulting firm, did I tell you? Labor negotiations, contracts and such in the construction business. I got a bunch of morons working for me."

My head hurts. I switch the phone to my other ear. "Please?" I say.

"Oh, what the hell," Kopanski says. "Hey, Reilly," he calls. "Your son wants to know why you won't let him visit." I hear my father's bass rumble respond, but I can't make out what he's saying. "He says because he doesn't want to talk to you."

"Why doesn't he want to talk to me?" Kopanski asks. My father rumbles. "He says he doesn't want to talk about why he doesn't want to talk to you. Not in front of a stranger, he says. That's me."

"Tell him if he doesn't talk to me about why he doesn't want to talk to me, I'll never talk to him ever again."

"Are you kidding?"

"This is his last chance," I say. "Tell him."

Kopanski tells him. My father sounds like a ton of gravel rolling downhill. "He says you got some nerve," Kopanski says. "He says if you don't know why he won't talk to you, he sure as hell isn't going to be the one to tell you, but you could ask anybody who knows anything and they'll tell you that it's common knowledge that you've turned your wife and son against him."

"What?"

Kopanski sighs. "You either heard it or you didn't, kid."

"He's the one who turned them against him," I say. "He did it to himself."

"This is very sad," Kopanski says, "but basically I'm an uninterested party. You want my opinion, I think you and your father got a communication gap," and he hangs up.

I want to tell Kopanski to tell my father he's got *his* nerve. He's the one who came to me the morning of my wedding and told me I was making the biggest mistake of my life. And when I started law school, he's the one who told me he couldn't think of a scummier profession for a man to get into, unless it was grave robbing, maybe. And when Donny came along, he's the one who told us at every turn, for our own good of course, what a lousy job we were doing raising the boy: this week we were pampering him too much, making a little sissy out of him; next week we weren't showing him enough attention, he'd end up a little delinquent. One year: you mean to tell me that boy ain't potty trained yet? Another year: ease up, for chrissakes, let the boy learn to read at his own pace.

He's the one.

No wonder Kathy told him that last night he came to our place for dinner to shut up and mind his own goddamn business.

I want to tell Kopanski to tell my father all of this, but I'm out of change. I find a flower shop down the block, but the clerk won't give me change unless I buy something. I pick out a long-stemmed American Beauty.

"Will that be cash or charge, sir?"

"Give me a break."

While the clerk gets my change, a tiny white-haired lady in a rabbit coat comes in holding a shopping list in her liver-spotted hand. She stands next to me at the counter. "I need seven arrangements," she says, voice quivering. "One pink carnations in baby's breath, one yellow roses in baby's breath, one jonquils, whatever, in baby's—"

"Excuse me," I say. "I'm being waited on."

She stares at my paper-wrapped rose. "Excuse me, young man," she says, eyes misting, "but everybody I know is dying."

I go back to the phone booth. A middle-aged blonde woman in a maroon jogging suit is using it. I walk around the block looking for another booth. No luck. I return. Still there. I knock on the glass, point to my watch. She looks up, looks at my rose, grazes burgundy fingernails down the phone cord, continues talking. I rap on the glass. No response. I pound the booth with my fist. She jumps, stares at me.

"I've just been mugged," I shout. "My wife's lying in the street in a pool of blood. I have to call an ambulance."

She points to the hospital across the street, goes on talking. I pound on the booth again. She opens the door a crack.

"Do you mind?" she says, voice nasal and whining. "I can't hear my party."

"There's a fire down the street," I say. "My kitten's stuck in a burning tree. I have to call the fire department."

She rolls her eyes. "Some people," she says. "I'll call you back, honey." She jogs off without looking at me.

"Kopanski," Kopanski answers. "Who's this?"

"Kopanski, hang up on me one more time and I'm going to get twenty bucks worth of change and tie up your phone so bad your business will go straight down the tubes."

Silence.

"Did you hear me?"

"Who's this?" Kopanski says.

"Cut the crap."

"You got a personality problem, kid, anybody ever tell you that? You could use a Dale Carnegie course."

"Tell that stubborn old bastard he can go straight to hell. If he doesn't want to see me, fine, let him die a lonely old man."

Silence again.

"Go ahead, tell him," I say.

Kopanski's voice drops to a whisper. "Listen, son, I think you want to take it easy on your father just now. He's not looking too good, you know. I mean, a major injury like this at his age...."

"What are you saying?"

"His heart," Kopanski says, voice low and muffled. "I heard the doctors talking. This has been a big strain, the trauma, the surgery and all. They're saying maybe the old heart's not up to it. Even if he does come out of this okay, he's not going to be the same, he's going to need a lot of care. I shouldn't be telling you this, he didn't want you to know, said he didn't want you to worry or feel obliged to take him into your home and nurse him back to health or anything like that."

Now I'm silent.

"Kid?"

I clear my throat. "Tell him I have to talk to him."

"He's sleeping now," Kopanski says. "I don't think he should be disturbed. Tell you what, why don't you come here and see him."

"They won't let me. No visitors."

"Visit me, then," Kopanski says, and he hangs up.

I call Kathy, ask her how she'd feel about my father moving in with us.

"Please," she says, "please, please, please, please, no, honey, please, God, please."

The plump young nurse looks up from her terminal. "Oh, no," she says. "I told you, sir, your father specifically requested—"

"I'm here to see Mr. Kopanski. What room's he in?"

"Kopanski?"

"Kopanski."

She taps it out on her keyboard. "Room 243," she says, then frowns. "Wait a minute." She types some more. "That's your father's room."

"I'm not visiting my father. I'm visiting Mr. Kopanski, a very close and dear friend. You want to give me a hard time?"

She shrugs, hands me a visitor's pass. "Nice flower," she says. "Better put it in water before it dies."

I walk down the hall to 243, hoping nobody wheels past anybody bloody. The door is slightly ajar. I take a deep breath, knock, push it open. A small, leathery man lies in bed, buried from ankles to ribs in a cast. He looks up sharply.

"Mr. Kopanski?" I say.

"Who're you?"

"Michael Reilly."

"You look like a summons server." He squints. "Nice flower, though. Is that for me?"

I look around the room. The second bed is empty. "Where's my father?"

He stares at me, shakes his head. "Gone," he says.

"Gone?"

"Gone." He raises a skinny white arm, snaps his fingers. "Like that, son. Heart couldn't take it, I guess. Sorry."

My pulse jumps. "What are you talking about?"

"Sad piece of business," he says. "He called for you at the end, you know. Said tell that no good punk son of mine that where I'm going he still can't visit. Then he went like this—" Kopanski throws his head back, teeth bared and clenched, gurgles low in his throat, then lets all the air out slowly, eyes open wide, mouth gaping. I stare at him. After a moment, his eyes flicker and he lifts his head. "Croaked," he says. "Just like that. Nice that he thought of you at the end, though. You want to put that rose in water or what?"

I open my mouth, close it, open it again. "You son of a bitch," I say.

Kopanski smiles. "Had you going there for a second, didn't I. Touching, really, seeing that kind of filial concern."

"Where is he?"

"They took him down to X-ray, checking their work."

"You son of a bitch."

Kopanski's eyes flash. "That's enough of that, son. I'm not your old man. I don't put up with anybody talking to me like that. You get yourself some manners or you're out of here quicker than I can call the nurse to call security. Now maybe I shouldn't have kidded you like that, but I've never seen a harder case than you and your father, and I've seen some hard cases. I'm sick of you two, I don't mind telling you, him complaining about you and you complaining about him. Good Lord. Can't you think of something positive about him?"

"Not offhand. Can you?"

"Not my job. He's *your* father, kid, not mine. I buried mine seven years ago, and I can tell you, I still miss him." He looks away, clears his throat. "But that's not your business, and your business ain't my business. You got nothing good to say about your old man, fine. Pretty pitiful, if you ask me, but nobody asked me." He gives me an appraiser's squint. "Looks like you're doing all right for yourself. What do you need a father for?"

I think about this, anger simmering to embarrassment. Sure, my father's been a pain in the ass for years now, but he wasn't always that way. I think about how hard he worked when I was growing up, how he'd come home late at night, dirty and tired, and how he'd still pick me up in the air or after I was too big ruffle my hair and ask me all about my day and sit listening, really listening to me, as if my day were much more important than his own. I think about all the good times he gave me, weekends batting balls to me or teaching me to hammer and saw or taking Mom and me to the beach and letting us bury him in the sand until he was red-faced and giggling, begging us to dig him out. I think of a lot of good things, but the past ten years won't let me say them.

"Well?" Kopanski says.

"My mother loved him," I say, finally.

"Well," Kopanski says. "That's good. That's something."

"He loved her, too."

"Fine. That's the stuff. Think of that. Did you love your mother, by the way?"

I swallow, nod.

"Excellent. That's what's known in the trade as common

ground. Listen, your father should be back in a half-hour or so. I got a deck of cards in the top drawer. You wouldn't happen to know how to play canasta, would you? Your old man won't play gin rummy and I never even heard of his game."

I drag a chair up to the bed, begin explaining the rules. Forty minutes later I owe Kopanski just under thirty bucks when they wheel my father back in, cursing the nurse and the orderly for handling him too rough. He raps the cast on his left leg with his knuckles. "What're you trying to do," he's yelling, "break the damn thing again?"

He sees me, leans up on his elbows, full grey hair matted and tangled, eyes burning, face red. "What the hell?" he says. He looks at Kopanski. "What the hell is he doing here?"

Kopanski shrugs, smiles, begins whistling tunelessly.

I stand, pick up the rose from Kopanski's bedside table. It's beginning to wilt a bit. "I brought you this," I say.

He looks at it, looks at me, and for a moment I see a kind of uncertain panic in those eyes, the same kind I saw when he told me Mom had died in the middle of the night while he was gone for a cup of coffee from the hospital cafeteria. He sniffs, and the eyes burn again.

He turns to the orderly. "This is my son," he says. "I think I was telling you about him. Been a little down on his luck lately so he can't afford one of those nice ten-dollar arrangements."

A muscle jumps in my jaw. "Talk to me," I say. "I'm right here."

"Probably pulled that one from the neighbor's yard," he says. The orderly wheels the gurney next to his bed, and the nurse pulls down the sheets. "This may be a bit uncomfortable, Mr. Reilly," she says. "Try to relax when we move you."

Kopanski studies his cards. "Don," he says idly, "none of my business, but the kid's not a bad kid. Maybe you want to talk to him."

My father glares at him, then looks at me, eyes shining. I try to picture him with my mother, the way she'd serve his dinner and stand behind him with her hands on his shoulders until he took his first bite, the way they'd walk down the sidewalk hand-in-hand, my father touching the small of her back when they crossed the street.

The orderly and nurse lift and roll, and my father is deposited howling in bed.

"Dad," I say.

His teeth clench back the pain, his eyes shut tight, and I suddenly understand what he's afraid of. It's not death, not his own, anyway. That cantankerous heart will beat strong and hard until it bursts, and he'll gladly let it. I step towards him, arms outstretched, and he opens his eyes, lets them soften for a moment before he veils them with a snarl.

"I don't need you here," he says. "Go home."

I touch his trembling fist. Our eyes meet. His hand slowly opens, and I place the drooping rose in his palm. "You stupid son of a bitch," I say, voice hoarse. "You poor pigheaded son of a bitch."

"Well," I hear Kopanski say behind me. "At least they're talking."

Constrictor

Tommy's wife Lynne wanted a pet: a darling floppy-eared English cocker spaniel maybe, or maybe a blue-eyed Siamese cat, all arch and mysterious, or a goddamn goldfish even. Christ, she needed *some*body to talk to all day long.

Lynne had been out of work for nine weeks now and was going crazy, she claimed. She'd had this rewarding career as an assistant purchasing agent trainee for an automotive parts retailer until she came in late one morning, got chewed out by her boss again, finally told the tight-assed old bastard what she truly thought of him.

Now her life was empty and shitty, she complained, nothing to do all day every day but get up, make Tommy breakfast, kiss him goodbye, make the bed so she wouldn't be tempted to get back in it, exercise with the TV, clean up breakfast, start some laundry, watch some "Donahue" maybe.

Some excitement.

Afternoons she could vacuum, dust, read through the employment classifieds maybe, yellow highlighter poised mid-air, ready to circle the perfect career opportunity. Hah. Then on to

"General Hospital" while she thought of what to defrost for dinner.

Such options! What a rut. A pet would help, she said.

"How about a baby instead?" Tommy suggested.

Lynne's mouth hung open a moment. "It's not the same, Tommy."

Tommy shrugged, lowered his eyes. "Baby'd keep you company."

"Forget it."

"You said sooner or later."

They'd been married four years now. Before they'd tied the knot, back when they still talked about matters important to their future together, Lynne had said sure, she wanted to have kids sooner or later, two or three even.

"Sooner or later we will, probably," she said now. "If and when the time is right. This isn't the right time. I'm too young." Lynne was 24 years old. Tommy was only 27 but had begun to worry that if he didn't start a family soon he'd end up too old to play ball with his kids. "Besides," Lynne said, "we shouldn't have children until we work out the problem with our marriage."

Tommy nodded. He didn't agree that there *was* a problem with their marriage—other than the problem of Lynne's insisting on finding a problem with it—but he'd heard Lynne's side before and didn't much feel like hearing it again. According to Lynne, the *main* problem was that she and Tommy failed to communicate sufficiently to forge a healthy, happy, open, and equal partnership. One time Tommy called this notion "a pile of *Cosmo* crap," but that had started Lynne off. See? He never *listened*, they never com*mun*icated.

"Anyway," Lynne went on, "you're changing the subject. I want a pet."

Tommy considered the idea. "What happens if you find another job? Who'll take care of your pet then?"

Lynne lit a cigarette. She'd just started up after having quit for nearly six months. "I'm not a child," she said, spitting smoke dramatically. "I know a pet is a responsibility. But look at cats, they're independent, they take care of themselves. Dogs guard your house while you're away."

Well, Tommy didn't know. He didn't much care for dogs or cats, he told her, especially in an apartment. The hair, the noise, the smell. "No," Tommy told her. "We can't do dogs or cats."

Lynne frowned. "How about a canary?"

"Feathers. Bird crap."

"Hamster?"

Tommy studied this. "That's like a rat with no tail, right?"

Well, all right then, Lynne exploded. She wasn't about to infringe on his domain. No goddamn pet, all right. She'd just go crazy.

"Look," Tommy said, but Lynne turned away.

"Listen," Tommy said, but Lynne covered her ears.

"Come on," Tommy said, but Lynne wouldn't budge.

Tommy was stymied, felt like giving in and buying her an *ostrich* if she wanted. But no. Truth to tell, he didn't mind pets. There were always animals around the house when he was a kid. And though he thought it unfair to keep a pet cooped up in an apartment, it was no big deal. The big deal was, Tommy wanted babies. Now, as soon as possible, as many as Lynne would give him. And Tommy was afraid a pet would sap Lynne's motherly instincts, displace her natural longings so that, eventually, she wouldn't feel the *need* for kids. He'd seen it happen. Childless couples fussed over their pets, gushed over them, oohed and ahhed, pampered them, treated them like children. This, in Tommy's view, was nearly as bad as feeding your kids dog food.

"Our lease," Tommy announced suddenly, "says no pets."

"So what?" Lynne said. "Who cares?" she went on. "Who reads leases?" she insisted. "Allen has a pet."

Tommy rolled his eyes. "Allen's a jerk."

"Allen's my friend," Lynne said. "He listens to me, he understands me." She glared at Tommy. "He's not the one who's a jerk."

Allen had moved into an efficiency down the hall almost nine months ago. He was a graduate student at the university—philosophy, Tommy thought, or psychology or one of those. Tommy never bothered to ask. Allen bored the hell out of him.

But he didn't bore Lynne. Shortly after he'd moved in she bumped into him in the hall, ended up helping him clean up his apartment. It was the neighborly thing to do, she said. Next thing Tommy knew she'd invited Allen over for dinner. She felt sorry for him, she said. Poor guy, he lived all alone, studied till all hours, obviously wasn't eating right, he was so skinny. He just didn't look *healthy*, and his clothes were always wrinkled and baggy like he slept in them, and Tommy should see his apartment—mattress on the floor, cinder block bookshelves, card table for a desk. He really needed some friends, Lynne thought.

"Sounds like he needs a wife," Tommy said.

Looking grimly anemic, Allen arrived for dinner. Tommy offered him a beer. Allen declined, but sipped on a glass of grapefruit juice and soda. Lynne lit a cigarette. Allen snuffled, asked if she'd mind terribly not smoking. An allergy, it seemed. She really should think about quitting.

"Imagine your lungs," he said.

All through dinner—Tommy's favorite, corned beef and cabbage, which Allen barely touched and cut the fat off of when he did—Allen talked about psychology or philosophy or whatever, dropping names Tommy didn't recognize (with Lynne nodding along as though she did) and making pompous-sounding observations that Tommy found unfathomable in a dryly urbane manner that Tommy found increasingly annoying.

"How 'bout them Tigers?" Tommy said at one point.

Allen paused, blinked. "What tigers are those?"

"Detroit."

Allen blinked again.

Tommy leaned back in his chair, clasped his hands behind his head. "Follow much baseball, Al?"

"I'm afraid," Allen said, smiling slowly, "that I really don't see the point."

"Baseball's so boring," Lynne said. "Tommy's a nut for it though."

Allen arched an eyebrow. "Chacun a son gout."

"No shit," Tommy said.

Lynne giggled.

"Jesus," he told her after Allen left, "no wonder that guy doesn't have any friends."

But Lynne liked him. He was different, she said. He was funny. He was smart. She invited him back. She quit smoking. Tommy would come home from work and find notes from Lynne saying she was over at Allen's, she was helping Allen give his pet ferret Deirdre a bath, she and Allen had gone to the market.

"Should I be worrying about you guys?" Tommy asked her finally.

Lynne told him not to be ridiculous.

True, Tommy conceded, Allen was too ugly.

Lynne tilted her head. "He's not ugly," she said. "He's got a certain kind of appeal that's just hard for some people to see."

Tommy looked at her.

"You have nothing to worry about," she said, and she kissed him hard on the lips. "Thanks, though."

But now that Lynne was unemployed, she and Allen seemed to "bump into each other" quite regularly.

"Hey!" Lynne said the day after she'd brought up wanting a pet. "Maybe I ought to go back to school."

"What for?" Tommy said.

Lynne didn't know, a few classes, computers or history or something. "Allen says as long as I'm out of a job, I may as well do something useful with my life."

Tommy was thinking that as long as she was out of a job, she might as well have a baby. *That* was useful. But he didn't tell her this.

"Allen says I'm smart."

"Yeah?" Tommy said.

"Yeah. A couple of times he said that." Lynne grinned, head ducked, eyes raised and dancing. "Do you think I'm smart?"

"Sure," Tommy said. "You're pretty smart. Smarter than a lot of people, I guess."

Lynne nodded, smiling. "So if I'm so smart, how come I can't have a pet?"

"What's that got to do with anything?"

"Nothing," Lynne said, shrugging. "I just want one."

That weekend, Tommy took Lynne to the zoo. They ate popcorn and caramel apples and fed peanuts to the elephants. Lynne made faces at a yawning bear and held Tommy's hand, swinging it like a schoolgirl. Tommy roared at a tiger. They stood on the fringe of a crowd and watched a gorilla alternately pawing his genitals and scratching his nose.

"I think he's confused," she said, and she smiled brightly.

A hollow-eyed man leading a pregnant woman brushed past them, stopped, hugged the woman awkwardly, her belly like a watermelon pressed between them. She was crying. "I can't wait anymore," she was sobbing. "I want our baby *now*."

Tommy touched Celia's arm.

Her nose wrinkled. "The joys of pregnancy," she whispered.

In the snake house, they saw the giant anaconda, the colorful python, the hooded cobra. The air inside was wet and stifling. Lynne turned wicked, grinned like a little girl playing doctor behind her parents' garage, licked her lips, and, staring at a boa constrictor coiled long and slimy round the branch of a tree, rubbed her hand up Tommy's crotch.

"Honey," he whispered, "there's people around."

"Can't help it," she panted, winking. "It's so *big!*"

Tommy slapped her butt, and she danced away, laughing, teasing, as lively and lovely as he'd ever seen her.

Lynne was all right for a few days, but the next week she wouldn't stop talking about school.

"You hated school," Tommy told her one night over dinner.

True enough, though Lynne wouldn't admit it now. After high school, she'd finished three semesters at the university (chalking up a cumulative grade point average of 2.17) before dropping out to marry Tommy. She'd never declared a major. She just wasn't *interested* in anything there. School was stupid, she'd insisted when her parents tried to talk her into staying for a degree and letting them pay for it. College was dumb and boring, she'd told Tommy: he hadn't missed a thing.

Tommy tended to agree. What was the use? Some people just weren't meant for college. Tommy was no dope—his job in shipping and receiving down at the plant took a sharp memory for inventory and such, all kinds of complicated bills of lading to fill out, so forth—but he'd never had the patience for sitting in a classroom listening to some teacher drone on about God knew what.

He'd always figured Lynne was that way too.

"I didn't *hate* school," Lynne argued now. "It just wasn't right for me at the time. I was young, immature. I didn't know what I wanted in life."

"You knew you wanted to marry me."

Lynne nodded pensively. Tommy felt suddenly uncomfortable.

"We really can't afford it," he said.

But Lynne had it all figured out. Allen said she could get a student loan easy. Allen said she could work part time, take night classes even. Allen said there were grants she could get, depending on financial need.

"I don't know," Tommy said. "Sounds a little flaky to me, I guess."

Lynne put down her fork, a lump of leftover meatloaf impaled on its prongs. "What's so flaky about wanting to better myself?" she said. "I think the real reason you don't want me going to college is because *you* never went to college. You're afraid I'll get too smart."

Tommy rolled his eyes. "Allen say that too?"

Lynne froze. "Forget it," she said, voice tight and wavering. "Just forget it." She stood abruptly and left the table.

Tommy knocked on Allen's door the next morning before work. It took awhile, but Allen finally answered, bleary-eyed and smelling like stale Old Spice. He had a towel wrapped around his waist.

"Tommy," Allen said. "Hi."

"Look," Tommy said. "Knock it off with my wife, huh?"

"Excuse me?"

"Just knock it off."

Still, Lynne wouldn't let up. She'd forgotten about college, it seemed, but now she wanted to com*mun*icate all the time.

"You know," she said one evening while they lay on the sofa watching a movie on HBO, "I'm really beginning to worry about our relationship."

Tommy prayed to God she'd find a job soon.

"Please," he said. "I'm trying to watch this."

"I'm serious. We have to talk."

The movie was a comedy, all about this guy who loses his job, so he stays home taking care of the kids while his wife goes off to work. It was pretty funny. The wife's boss was trying to seduce her right now.

"Tommy?" Lynne said. She touched his arm.

"Okay. What's wrong with our relationship."

"I don't think we have an equal arrangement."

"Listen," Tommy said, jaw tight. "I worked my ass off today. I work my ass off every goddamn day." The guy's wife punched her boss in the nose, knocked him sprawling. "I don't know how serious you think you are, but I don't need this shit right now, okay?"

Ten minutes later, Lynne went to bed without a word, without even kissing him goodnight. Tommy stayed up and watched the end of the movie. The guy and his wife still loved each other: the guy got his old job back and the wife quit hers.

Tommy joined Lynne in bed, snuggled up to her back. He felt her stiffen.

"You awake?" Tommy said.

"I am now."

"Let's talk it over."

"Talk *what* over," she said. "There's nothing to talk about. You don't want me to do what I want to do," she said. "That's all."

Tommy apologized: sure he wanted her to do what she wanted to do; he just wasn't sure *she* knew what she wanted to do. Lynne said of *course* she knew what she wanted to do. Tommy said what, go to college, buy a dog, communicate, what.

Lynne turned over, looked him hard in the eyes. "I have to do something, Tommy. Maybe I can't know what it is until I do it."

Tommy shook his head.

"Don't laugh at me," Lynne said.

"I'm not laughing at you, honey."

"You're being condescending. Allen says—"

"Fuck Allen," Tommy shouted.

He heard Lynne let her breath out slowly, saw her bottom lip tremble and then tighten. She flipped over, punched her pillow.

"You're the boss," she said.

"Hey," Tommy said. "Hey, I'm sorry."
Lynne lay rigid. "I know," she said.

Tommy lay awake for some time, thinking. Lynne had been such a joy when first they'd met, all dark-eyed and wild and full of mischief. On their second date they'd ended up skinny-dipping at an abandoned quarry where she ran from him, giggling, and dove cleanly and surfaced silently, black hair fanning in the water and flying sleek and dripping when she thrashed upward to splash him.

But the wildness, the willfulness had turned to selfish bitching and grousing. Or maybe he wasn't being fair. He loved her now, he knew, but maybe not as much, not as intensely, not as *joyfully* as he used to.

A baby would help. A baby would be someone to sacrifice for. A baby would give him something sweet and new and beautiful to love about her again.

Tommy propped himself on his elbow, faced Lynne's long, gently stirring back. He kissed her shoulder. Her breathing remained slow and even. He kissed her again.

"Goodnight," he told her.

The following afternoon, Tommy told his foreman he had to leave early. His foreman gave him a hard time at first—they had three trucks lined up waiting to be unloaded—but Tommy told him that the future of his marriage was at stake, and his foreman, a good family man himself, relented.

On the way home, Tommy stopped at the mall, found a pet shop. Tommy saw the usual fare—dogs, cats, fish, guinea pigs, birds—as well as a more exotic collection: mynah birds and parrots, startlingly vivid and chatty; sharp-eyed monkeys, sage and all-to-human looking for his tastes; a fuzz-pawed leopard litter playfully batting each other about; and one big snake.

Tommy stared at the sliding creature. It moved slowly, gathering motion from its tail and undulating it forward. It slithered, coiling and uncoiling, behind the glass of a large terrarium. Tommy tapped on the glass. The snake froze, eyed his finger, drew back its head with quick little jerky movements, flicked its tongue.

Here was an animal, Tommy concluded, that could never be mothered.

A short blonde sales clerk approached, asked if she could help.

"Yeah," Tommy said. "What kind of snake is this?"

She bent to read the three-by-five index card taped to the glass. Her hair was done up in a loose bun, and Tommy stared at the wispy-fine down on the back of her neck.

"Boa constrictor, sir," the sales clerk read. "From the Bahamas. One-point-eight meters long."

"What's that in feet?"

The clerk straightened up. "A lot of snake." She smiled. "I don't do metric."

Tommy laughed, flirting a bit. He didn't know quite what to ask next but felt compelled to ask something. You don't buy a boa constrictor every day. "Is it male or female?" he said.

She looked at Tommy, looked at the snake, looked back at Tommy. "Want me to check?"

Tommy guessed it didn't matter. "Wrap it up," he said.

Tommy was buying on a whim, he realized—he knew nothing about snakes, wasn't sure Lynne would care for it at all—but he bought two books—*Our Reptilian Friends* and *How to Build Your Very First Vivarium*—and figured that if Lynne didn't like it, he could always bring it back, trade it in on a terrier or something. Whatever she wanted.

"What about you?" he asked the sales clerk as she rang up his order. "Could you love a man who bought you a snake?"

She shrugged. "I read something in the paper one time about a guy who got eaten by his pet anaconda." She smiled sweetly. "I think the trick is to keep them happy and well-fed."

Tommy stared at her. "Worked here long?" he asked, finally.
"Seven weeks," she said. "This was my first snake."

On the way home, snake safely burlap-bagged in the back seat, Tommy felt excited. He imagined Lynne's reaction to her new pet. He saw her squealing with shock and delight, hugging and kissing him. *Oh, how did you know,* she'd say. *Just what I always wanted.* The snake was worth a smile at least. He imagined her naming it: Bobby the Boa, Connie Constrictor. He pictured her taking it for a slither down the street.

He liked the idea.

But when he got home, Lynne wasn't there. No note on the refrigerator, though she wouldn't be expecting him home this early. He took the snake out of the bag, draped it around his neck, tried to get used to the cool slowly-rolling weight of it.

An hour later, two hours before Tommy usually got home, Lynne still hadn't returned. Tommy was used to the snake now, spoke to it with gruffly affectionate impatience. Where was she? Afternoon off and what happens? Got a goddamn snake and no goddamn wife to give it to. The snake hung over Tommy's shoulders, tail end coiled once about his right arm, head lifted and tongue flicking with a dry ticking sound by his left ear. Periodically Tommy slowly turned his head to the left to see the serpent eye to eye. Probably out shopping with Allen or something.

Finally, Tommy got too itchy to wait any longer. He crossed the hall, snake still draped around his neck, figuring he'd check with Allen first, see if he'd seen her or what. He could hear music playing from inside Allen's apartment, some kind of third-world jazz, the kind where four or five musicians play four or five different melodies on four or five different instruments all at the same time. A cymbal crashed, saxophone farted, Tommy knocked. Waited. Knocked. The music stopped. Then Tommy heard someone whisper something, and the music started up again. He knocked.

The door opened partway and Allen peeked out from around it. He was dressed in a short beige terrycloth robe, and his knobby knees bumped the doorframe.

"Oh," Allen said. He looked like he'd just woken up. "Jesus," he said, "what the hell is that?"

"Snake," Tommy said. "Seen Lynne?"

"Who?"

"Lynne."

Allen stared at him blankly. "What are you doing with a snake?"

"It's a gift. It's for Lynne. She wants a pet."

Allen frowned. "She'll love it, I'm sure."

"Have you seen her?"

"Isn't she at home?"

There was a scrabbling sound: Tommy looked down: the ferret clawed at Allen's ankles. "Stop it, Deirdre," Allen said. He stooped to pick up the animal. Tommy peered into the drab little apartment: mattress on the floor; a folding card table in the corner covered with books and papers; stove, sink, and fridge jammed in a tiny alcove; bathroom door closed, light shining through the crack at the bottom. Allen stood, stroked the ferret's dirty white fur.

"No, she's not at home," Tommy said. "That's why I'm looking for her. I thought maybe you'd seen her."

The ferret was yipping and growling now, clawing its way up Allen's robe; Tommy felt the snake's weight shifting across his shoulders. "Shoosh, now Deirdre!" Allen commanded. He was looking at Tommy. "Your snake is scaring her. I haven't seen Lynne. I mean, I saw her earlier today, but I think she went shopping." The ferret snarled. Allen winced. "I mean, she said she might go shopping later. She'll probably be home soon. You're home early, aren't you?"

"Yes," Tommy said. "I'm home early."

The ferret jumped then, raking Allen's neck, fell to the floor, and ran yipping onto the bed. Allen cursed, slammed the door shut. And Tommy stood staring at the closed door, felt the snake's head pressing against his cheek, the tongue darting.

Tommy went back to his apartment. He put the snake in the bathtub, left it sliding across the porcelain, closed the door behind him. Then he sat on the sofa and waited. A half hour later Lynne breezed in, face flushed, smiling.

"You're home early," she said.

"I know. I brought you a present."

"Really? What is it?"

"It's in the bathroom," Tommy said. "I think you're going to like it."

"In the *bath*room," Lynne said, smiling uncertainly. "What is it, a new toilet bowl cover?"

"You'll see," Tommy said. "It's a surprise. Go ahead, go see."

"You're such a mystery man," Lynne said, but she walked off towards the bathroom, hesitating only slightly, Tommy thought, when her hand touched the doorknob.

Zoo Welcomes New Arrival

Maybe it's the combination of changes in his life—starting a new job, moving downtown, Celia getting pregnant, all in the first year of their marriage—but Casey hasn't been sleeping well lately.

It doesn't help that the city is suffering record-high temperatures, either. What with the hazy sun baking the streets all day and no air conditioning in their two-story row house, Casey and Celia have been sleeping with the bedroom windows open, and all the noises outside filter up and in through the whirring box fan. Bottles breaking, drunks raging, sirens shrieking, kids screaming: these things startle Casey out of sleep. Quiet, ghostly voices drift by, discussing lives Casey has no part in: they nag him awake.

Meanwhile, Celia sleeps through damn near anything. Fitfully, at times, now that she's into her third trimester and can't seem to toss and turn her way into a position comfortable enough to last her ten minutes on end, but she sleeps. Casey lies awake next to her, waiting for her to stir and settle, listening for more noises from the street.

"What singing?" she says in the morning when Casey complains of some wino glee club on the corner that kept him awake half the night. "What gunshots?" she says, when they sounded so close his heart only stopped stuttering after he pulled his aluminum softball bat from beneath the bed, felt its reassuring weight tight in his grip. "Probably just a car backfiring," she says, massaging a sleepless night's stiffness from his neck. "My man, weapon in hand, protecting hearth and home. Relax," she says. "We're safe."

One night a street gang on the corner laughs and curses and shouts so loudly that even Celia wakes up.

"I'm calling the police," Casey says.

City girl born and bred, Celia's skeptical. "Cops can't do much but chase them off, and they'll come back and make more trouble when they find out somebody complained."

Casey calls the police.

"We can send somebody around in an hour or so," the desk sergeant tells him, "but I'll be honest, sir, we're very busy tonight and this is not a priority call unless you want to file a formal complaint, in which case you'd have to appear at a hearing, and God knows what kind of retribution some of these kids might plan for you and your family once they know who you are and where you live. I hope you understand me."

"Relax," Celia tells him. "You have to learn to live with street noises, kind of like living by a waterfall."

A bottle shatters; a girl screams high and shrill, laughs wildly.

"Close the window if you want," she says. "You'll get used to it."

But it's too hot to close the window and Casey knows he'll never get used to the street.

Last year, right after they were married, when they were looking for a place to live, Casey suggested a country house he knew twenty minutes outside the beltway that needed caretaking. They'd get free rent in return for mowing a few acres of unused pastureland, feeding a dozen or so chickens, keeping the house clean and in good repair.

"Who has time for that?" Celia said. "We both work."

"It's not much, really. We could handle the chores on weekends."

"What do we know about farms?"

"It's not a farm. This is horse country, Celia."

"So what does a boy from the suburbs know about horses?"

"There aren't any horses. They don't use this place anymore."

She shook her head. "I couldn't live in the country. Too spooky. All alone out there like that?" She hugged his waist, ducked her head into his chest, shivered dramatically. "You ever see *In Cold Blood?*"

Instead she wanted to look at a bargain-basement-priced seventy-year-old row house just east of downtown in an area Casey would have thought twice about *driving* through let alone *living* in.

"It's the perfect starter house," Celia explained. "It's cheap, it's in decent shape, it's a step away from gentrification. Trust me. I know for a fact the gay community's got an eye on this neighborhood. Five years from now there'll be health food shops and gift boutiques on every corner. They'll strip the street and sandblast the original cobblestone. It'll be a showplace, believe me, I heard them talking about it at the office. This place is a renovator's dream. Tear up the linoloeum and we have hardwood floors, some paint and polish here and there and we can sell for three times what we buy for."

Besides, the location was a short bus ride, no transfer, to Celia's office downtown where she worked as a receptionist for one of the more successful real estate agencies in town.

So they bought.

And now Casey drives an hour each way in rush hour traffic to and from the manufacturing plant in the suburbs where he works in computer aided design, doodling out low-tolerance specifications for machining little parts of defense industry products he never sees. Mornings he picks his way through the trash on the street, unlocks his car, locks it behind him as soon as he's in. Evenings he parks his car as close as he can, walks briskly to his door, head down, avoiding eye contact with any of the bums and street punks who are starting to come alive with the setting sun.

One evening, as he locks his car, he sees a half-a-dozen teenagers loitering on the sidewalk a couple of houses down from his. They're laughing, smoking, passing around a paper-bagged bottle. Don't they have parents? he thinks. One girl, no more than thirteen or fourteen, lounges against an older boy, her thumb hooked in his back pocket, her fingers spread across the cheek of his ass. They look at him as he approaches. The older boy tilts his head, says something too low for Casey to hear, and the whole group snickers.

"Nice car," one of them calls, and they all grin at him like piranha. Casey nods in their direction, tries to smile, turns to his front door. Hands tremble, breath comes short, and the piercing laughter behind him reddens his neck as he unlocks three locks, enters, locks three locks, throws two deadbolts, latches a chain. He takes a deep breath.

"I'm home," he calls.

The next morning his tape player is gone, wires snaking out of the hole in the dashboard.

"You shouldn't park on the street," Celia says.

"There's no place else to park."

"Maybe we can rent a garage somewhere." She looks at her watch, kisses him quickly. "My poor baby, I'm late for work. Better report this to the police before you go."

"What's the use? They'll never get it back."

"Insurance report."

"Oh," Casey says, but he doesn't bother calling the police or replacing the tape player. The hum of tire on pavement is his only music this summer.

"Oh!" Celia says one night, sitting up suddenly in bed. "That was a big one."

Casey opens bleary eyes.

"He kicked me," Celia says. "Feels like he's playing soccer in there. Want to feel?" She grabs his hand, places it hard against her rounded belly. "Wait. He stopped. Wait a minute."

Casey waits, yawns, waits. "There," he says finally. "I felt it."

"No, that was me. Wait."

He toys with the line of coarse, dark hairs that have recently sprouted below her navel, takes his hand away to rub his eyes.

"There!" she says, grabbing his hand again. "That was a whopper. Did you feel it?"

"Missed it."

"Wait, he'll do it again."

Casey waits and waits. Suddenly her stomach bulges and rolls beneath his hand. He still can't get over how strange it feels, like holding a live fish in a plastic bag full of water.

"Wow," Celia says, "he's doing back flips. Did you feel it?"

"Yes, I felt it."

"Isn't that wild, how hard he kicks?"

Casey pats her stomach. "High point of my night."

"Well, you don't have to be so sarcastic."

"I'm just tired, honey, please." Casey rolls over, closes his eyes. "I love you, I love our baby, I need some sleep, okay?"

"Okay." Celia snuggles up to his back. "Sorry for waking you."

"You didn't wake me," Casey says.

As the summer wears on, it gets to the point where even when the street *is* quiet, even when he *does* fall off to sleep, he dreams he's awake, sweating, nagged by a muggy, cramped oppressiveness. He dreams that Celia's leg is draped heavy over both of his, that her arm coils around his throat like a boa constrictor, squeezing the breath out of him, that her swollen belly presses skin-to-skin tight against his ribs, that the baby is kicking, kicking at him.

He awakens hanging half off the bed, Celia wedged hard against him, a wealth of vacant mattress to the other side of her. He lifts her arm from his chest, slides out from beneath her leg, gets up, walks around to the other side of the bed, gets in. The sheets are cool beneath him. He stretches out, closes his eyes, listens to the street a minute or two before he hears her whimper in her sleep like a child denied, feels her weight shift, her body roll until it finds him again.

He kids her about it the next morning, her hogging the bed.

"Do I really?" she says, eyes wide, head tilted. "Come on, I don't do that, do I?"

He smiles. "You snore, too."

"Oh, come on, I do not," she says, grinning and blushing, delighted with her own mischief. "Do I?"

"What's the matter?" his boss says one afternoon. "Too much partying last night?"

Casey blinks at his screen, tries to bring the blurry curving green lines into focus. He's been revising the design of a cylindrical casing since lunch, rotating it this way and that on its axis, looking for the right perspective. He moves his stylus on the menu board.

"Oops," his boss says, leaning over his shoulder. "That doesn't belong there, does it?"

"No," Casey says. "I don't know," he says. "What I'm trying to do, I guess," he says, and forgets what he's trying to do. "I've been under a lot of pressure lately," he says, and wishes immediately he hadn't.

His boss's face softens. "Hey, that's okay. This part isn't critical. I'll give it to somebody else."

"At home," Casey says quickly. "I mean at home. We're having our first baby pretty soon, you know, my wife and I."

"Hey, that's right, congratulations, I forgot to tell you." He puts a hand on Casey's shoulder. "When's she due?"

"End of the summer."

"Sure picked a hot one. Well, hey, that's just wonderful. Best of luck to you both." He slaps Casey's back. "Listen, hey, I know what you're going through, but appreciate your time together now, a baby doesn't give you a minute's rest. Believe you me, I know, I got four of my own. They take up all your time. Me and my wife used to hire a sitter and rent a room at the Holiday for the evening, just to get some peace and quiet sometimes." He laughs. "You think you got pressure now, wait'll the midnight feedings start, wait'll the potty training starts, wait'll the first day of school. Are you in a good school district?"

"I don't know," Casey says. "I don't think so."

"Where do you live again?"

Casey tells him.

His boss frowns. "None of my business, but I don't even know if they *have* schools there. No offense, it's your life, but I wouldn't raise a *dog* in that part of town. Believe you me, that is *not* a safe place for children. Believe you me," he says, and he walks off shaking his head.

The instructor of their childbirth class at the hospital downtown tells all the daddies to be especially patient with the mommies during the final month of pregnancy. "Mommy is feeling cranky right now, Daddy," the instructor says. "It's hot and sticky, and Mommy is feeling terribly blue. Take Mommy someplace nice, Daddy. Go dancing, get out of the house, go to the beach, get some fresh air. Mommy needs to get her mind off her body."

Casey suggests a picnic in the country somewhere, a state park, maybe, or maybe just some open meadowland off some winding back road.

"Let's go to the zoo," Celia says. "I haven't been to the zoo since

I was a kid. I read in the paper they have a new baby gorilla there. They say it looks just like a human baby, almost."

Casey heads for the car when they hit the street, but Celia stops him. "You and that car," she says. "Don't you get sick of driving? Let's take the bus."

A couple of bums are dozing in the kiosk at the end of their block—taking a break from a hard morning's begging, Casey figures—so he steers Celia up the street to the next stop. The bus driver smiles at Celia, lurches off while Casey's still counting out change. Celia grabs the handrail to keep from falling.

"Hey," Casey says sharply. "She's *preg*nant."

The driver shrugs. "So?"

"So be careful."

"Sure," the driver says.

"If she fell and hurt herself or the baby—"

"Okay, okay, sit down, Jesus."

"Forget it Casey, come on," Celia says, and she leads him unsteadily to a seat.

At the zoo, Casey buys two popcorns, one plain, one caramel, and though the animal stench is strong in the afternoon heat, the sun brings color to Celia's high, plump cheeks, and she laughs and flirts with him as they walk hand in hand.

"Apple cheeks," Casey tells her. "They look so good I want to take a bite out of one." He nips at her and she squeals and jumps like a skittish kitten.

There's a crowd at the gorilla cages. Celia squeezes her way through, pulling Casey behind her. "Pregnant lady," she says. "Excuse me, mother with child." People mostly smile and laugh as they move aside, though Casey hears a high school girl mumble, "I'm sure, like I care a *lot*," to her gum-chewing companion, who looks sideways at Casey and rolls her eyes.

Mother and daughter gorillas have a cage to themselves. Mother gorilla sits in the back corner, rocking her daughter in one arm and picking at her coat of fine brown fuzz. She eats what she picks. Baby gorilla sucks her thumb, eyes darting wide and wild from face to face outside the cage. Casey meets the eyes for a moment, but they quickly move on. The crowd behind them presses and jostles; a tall man to Casey's right, camera hanging from sunburnt neck, jabbers loudly in high-pitched monkey chatter: the baby gorilla twists her head, eyes moving, moving.

"God," Celia breathes. *"She's adorable."*

The tall man snorts. "Got a face only a mother could love."

Celia looks at him, dark eyes burning. "Asshole," she says.

Casey pulls her from the crowd, hugs her, rubs her back. He wipes the tears from her eyes.

"Casey, I can't wait anymore," she says. "I want our baby *now.*"

"Shoosh," he tells her. "It's okay, that's all right."

"The joys of pregnancy," he hears someone say behind him, and he turns to see a sharp-faced woman with long black hair smirking at them. The big dumb-looking guy holding her by the arm lowers his head, shrugs, lets her lead him away.

There are people in this world, Casey realizes, who should never have children. There are people who make this world a shitty place to bring children into.

Casey hugs Celia closer, stares into the cage behind her. A hulking male gorilla rocks on his haunches in the corner, scratches his groin, peers through the chain-link mesh separating him from mother and daughter gorillas in the adjacent cage. Casey knows that gorillas only *look* human, but he can't help noticing a sad, almost wistful expression on the ape's face.

"Hey!" he says, turning Celia around and pointing. "Do you think he might be the father?"

She wipes her eyes, grins suddenly. "How can you say a thing like that?" she says, winking. "Trust me, you're the father."

Casey laughs loud and long, sinks to his knees. He wraps his arms around her wide, full hips and nuzzles her belly, telling her how much he loves her again and again. Celia giggles—*Casey, people are watching*—but he doesn't care. She pushes him away, laughing and blushing and as beautiful as he's ever seen her.

"Control yourself!" she says. "That's the kind of wild passion that got us into trouble in the first place."

"No trouble," Casey says. "My pleasure."

And for the rest of the day, as they stroll from cage to cage, Casey can't keep his hands off her, as though she might slip out of sight, out of his life, if he's not touching her. He finds himself smiling mawkishly at babies in strollers, trading due dates and Lamaze tips with other pregnant couples, bragging about the force of his baby's kicks, and feeling proud, so proud and happy that he doesn't want the day to end.

That night, after they've made love—slowly, patiently, carefully, at first, and then more and more recklessly—and after Celia has talked herself to sleep counting off all the things that still need to be done before the baby comes—the nursery needs painting, the crib they bought last month must be put together, they still have to buy a car seat—Casey lies on his side staring at Celia. Suddenly her belly rolls. Casey puts his hand beneath her nightgown, feels the warm bulge moving, turning, kicking. It won't be long, he thinks. And the more he thinks it, the less the thought scares him, until, like a mantra, it soothes him to sleep.

"So why didn't you?" a sharp voice says.

Casey springs up in bed.

"I was going to," a girl's voice says. "I was all ready to."

"So why didn't you?"

"I don't know."

"You don't know," the first voice says, and Casey recognizes now that it's the voice of a boy trying to sound like a man. The boy curses, and Casey hears a sharp slap, the girl crying out. His skin prickles, and he reaches for his bat. Another slap. Casey gets out of bed, turns off the fan, takes it out of the window, and peers down at the street. On the sidewalk just below, a tall lean boy in sneakers, torn jeans, and a tank-top tee-shirt holds a girl by the arm. He shakes her. She lowers her head, doesn't resist. The streetlight down the block casts vague shadows, but Casey thinks he's seen these two before with the rest of their gang on the corner.

"You don't know," the boy's saying over and over, his voice rising to a mean, mocking falsetto now. He releases her, curses again, spits. "What's to know?" he says. "You go to the clinic, you get rid of it. What'd you do with the money?"

"I still got the money. I can still go."

"When?"

No answer.

"Casey?" Celia says behind him.

"Something's going on outside," he says.

"Come back to bed."

"There's some kids fighting down there."

"Close the window. Come to bed."

"When?" the boy shouts. He curses, holds the girl by the front of her shirt now, raises a fist, then pulls her sharply towards him.

"Please," she says, crying.

"Don't please me! What are you trying to do to me?"

"Hey!" Casey shouts, and the boy jumps, looks up.

"Hey what?" the boy shouts back, dark face gleaming in the soft light. Long lean muscles bunch and gather. "Hey *what!*" he screams up at the night.

Casey's heart jumps. "Knock it off," he calls down, and the weakness of his voice angers him.

The boy curses, curses, curses, vile raging nonsensical curses, threats, curses that make Casey back away from the window.

"Don't!" the girl says, and the boy suddenly swings at her, knocks her to the ground. "Is this what you want?" he says, voice shaking. "Is this what it takes?"

And Casey feels the heat surge from his chest to his head, his throat tightening, his grip burning the bat. He pulls on a pair of jeans, Celia telling him no, no, Casey, wait, I'll call the police, don't go, but it's too late now as Casey races down the stairs. He pulls open the front door, slams it tight behind him.

The girl lies on the sidewalk, moaning. The boy stands beside her, fists raised, tears streaming down his face.

"Leave her alone," Casey says.

"Stay out of this!" The boy grabs the girl by the arm, yanks her to her knees. "Let's go," he says, but she slumps to the ground. He yanks her up again. "Come *on!*"

"Enough!" Casey yells, bat raised.

The boy turns to him, eyes wild. "You want some of this?" He whirls suddenly and punches her, knocks her sprawling against the house, and Casey feels a growling bellow of fear and hate rising in his throat to a roar as he springs forward swinging and the bat connects. The boy falls and rolls, holding his shoulder, howls and howls, cries no, no, no in a high, heartbreaking whine that reminds Casey that this is, truly, just a boy, a child made of fragile bone and fledgling muscle.

"God," Casey says. "Oh, hey." He drops the bat, aluminum ringing on asphalt, and kneels to touch him, but the boy twists away, struggles to his feet, and stumbles off down the block, left arm hanging limp, the high, rasping sounds of his weeping fading as he turns the corner.

"Casey," Celia calls from above. "Please come in. I called the police. Casey, please!"

"In a minute," he says. He walks to the girl, helps her up. "Are you all right?"

She won't look at him.

"Hey," he says. "You want to come in? You want to go to the hospital?"

She pulls back. "What are you doing here?" she says. "What do you want?"

Casey stands awkwardly, still panting. He's shirtless, shoeless, and suddenly doesn't know what to do with his hands. "I live here," he says. "I heard the trouble."

The girl shakes her head. "You don't know the trouble."

Casey takes a deep breath, hooks his thumbs in his belt loops. "I live here," he says, voice surer now. "He woke my wife. My wife needs her sleep. My wife's pregnant."

The girl looks up towards the second floor, dark eyes troubled, a purple blotch rising on her cheek, and she folds her hands across her stomach. Casey follows her gaze to where Celia stands in the window, hands pressed against the screen, crying low and soft.

"Casey, please, it's starting, I need you, it's starting."

"What's starting?"

"Contractions."

But it's too early, Casey knows, the baby's not due till end of summer, they'll have to weather the heat before they come to term. "You're kidding," he says.

"Casey, I mean it."

He feels the girl watching him, but when he looks at her, she turns away, begins walking slowly down the sidewalk.

"We can take you to the hospital," he calls after her, and a short convulsive giggle escapes him. "We're going anyway."

She glances back, tears shining in the streetlight's glow, looks back up to the window. Then she turns the corner and is gone.

Do what you want, Casey thinks. Just a child, the both of them, children left out to roam the night. The night is no time for children, no time at all, too dangerous, too stifling, too dark. It's just too late, he thinks, as he hears the door open behind him and turns to see Celia framed in the doorway, hands supporting the weight of her belly, teeth clenched and eyes narrowed to slits. She lets out a gasp, a whimper. "Jesus," she says. "What a night to start this."

Casey reaches for her. "Don't be scared," he says softly. "We're safe now. It's all over."

Baby Gets Ouchy

Mommy and Daddy are new to this: he's twenty-five and she twenty-two when the first little bundle of wide-eyed love and dreams comes their way. Feet still trembling in the stirrups, Mommy arches forward to where baby lies wrinkled and bloody on Mommy's wobbly tummy, presses her nose to baby's plastered black hair.

"God," Mommy says. "Smell."

Daddy's eyes blur. He pulls down the surgical mask, bends toward his daughter, fills himself with the faint and musty-fresh aroma of charcoal and newfallen leaves. Nurse touches his arm, points at his dangling mask.

"Infection," she cautions.

First few days, all is well. Friends and family sigh and coo, show baby delightful gifts: seven rattles, two squeaky ducks, three pairs of pink booties. Mommy and Daddy make baby's nursery a wonderland of sunshine and tinkling music, make baby marvelous promises. Mommy will put off graduate school for baby. Daddy will work harder and longer, get job promotion for baby. Daddy will quit smoking for baby. Mommy will try religion again, get baby baptized. All eyes and open-minded expression, baby surveys her world, seems to understand.

Then baby gets ouchy.

One week old and crying, crying all the livelong day, crying through the tiresome night. Break for a suckle at Mommy's breast then cry. Wake from an hour or so of sleep then cry. Dr. Spock is consulted. Bubble burped? Diaper pin? Hungry? Full? Wet? Chafed? Cold? Hot? *What?* Mommy tells Daddy don't force the pacifier on her if she doesn't want it. Daddy tells Mommy don't rock her so fast. Baby cries and cries.

Mommy calls pediatrician. Pediatrician listens, says *hum.* Temperature? No. Diaper rash? Nope. Milk enough? You bet. Stool soft? Yup. Stomach hard and bulgy like a grapefruit? That's the first thing Mommy checked for, doctor, but no sign of colic and *still* baby keeps crying. Pediatrician tisks: a little gas, probably, not to worry nor cause for alarm, do call if it goes on.

"Babies get ouchy sometimes," pediatrician says.

Mommy gets ouchy. Hormones won't leave her alone, make her feel pasty, bloated and blue all the livelong day. Episiotomy stings; stitches stab; boobies ache; baby cries.

Mommy knew baby wouldn't be easy, but Mommy never dreamed baby would be so *hard.*

Mommy always wanted baby, *always,* but Mommy didn't know she'd get ouchy baby, squirming and crying, voice thin and sharp sleepless nights on end now. But it's okay: Mommy loves her baby, yes she does, she does. Mommy worries, but it's okay, yes it is. Is baby hungry? Is baby tired? Is baby hurt or frightened or unhappy or what? It's okay, that's all right, Mommy kisses her baby and loves her baby and tells her so half the livelong day.

Daddy gets ouchy. Hard work fills each day, everybody telling him what to do. Evenings Daddy does what everybody tells him daddies are supposed to do: give poor mommies a break. Daddy should play with baby. Daddy should change baby's diaper.

Daddy should let Mommy try to take a little nap, she's so beat. Daddy should make dinner, clean up after. Later, Daddy should be very quiet in bed, careful not to disturb the blissfully gentle breathing from the basinet. Daddy should rub Mommy's aching back, lull Mommy off to sweet, sweet sleep, while Daddy lies awake waiting for the slightest whimper.

Middle of the night, baby wakes crying. Mommy feeds. Baby naps ten minutes, cries.

"Oh, honey, please?" Mommy moans. "I can't take another night."

Bleary-eyed, Daddy carries baby to the nursery, lays baby fussing and squirming on the changing table. He takes off baby's diaper, checks for rash. No sign. No surprise. Mommy and Daddy change baby's diaper damn near sooner than she wets it. Daddy powders baby's pink little palm-sized butt, jabs himself with a safety pin, doesn't cry out. Daddy mustn't cry out.

Baby still cries.

Daddy carries baby downstairs, through the living room, dining room, kitchen, back to the living room. He cradles baby, sways to and fro.

"Sleep," he tells her. "Sleep, my baby. Shoosh," he tells her. "Daddy's here."

Still baby cries. Daddy wonders what's the matter. Hate your job? Boss got you down? Lovelife souring? Bills piling up? Growing up too fast? Shoosh-a-bye my baby, Daddy's here. Daddy loves you. Yes he do, indeedy-doody-dee.

Baby wails.

Daddy gets scared. Daddy's heart races. Daddy's heart hasn't raced like this since he and Mommy were in the labor room where he sat on the edge of her bed through hours and hours of uncertain coaching—in-two-three-four, pant-pant-pant-*blow*— while Mommy turned her back on him, then clung desperately to his neck, trading her sour breath for his. Once, Mommy's eyes rolled, hips bucked, and suddenly she glared narrowly at him as though she might hate him. Daddy felt like crying then, but Daddy didn't cry until Mommy got into the delivery room and gasped and pushed and held her breath and whimpered and pushed and strained and baby's knobby little head squeezed through while Daddy stood by helplessly awestruck.

Then baby cried, Mommy cried, and Daddy cried, too.

Just like Daddy's crying now, baby cradled close to his face. Daddy's tears drip *plash* on baby's cheek, and Daddy and baby cry some more. Soon Mommy comes downstairs, face tipping this way and that.

"What's wrong?" she says, voice high and tight.

Daddy just shakes his head, crying. Mommy begins to cry too, wraps her arms around her Daddy and baby, all crying, crying. They sob, they sup-sup, they work themselves up in pitch, each outwailing the other. At first, Mommy and Daddy fight the tears—they tremble and sniffle and wipe each other's eyes—but after a while the crying comes easily, and it seems to Mommy and Daddy that they could go on crying for days, months, years, for the rest of baby's life, even. But they don't.

They only go on crying until baby finally stops.

Pat Rushin's stories have appeared in *The North American Review, Indiana Review, Kansas Quarterly, Quarterly West*, and in *Sudden Fiction: American Short Short Stories*. He lives with his wife and daughters near Orlando, where he teaches creative writing at the University of Central Florida.

OTHER GALILEO BOOKS

Inventions in a Grieving House, a novella by Patricia Grossman
Days of Summer Gone, poetry by Joe Bolton
The Octopus Who Wanted to Juggle, a children's story by
Robert Pack, illustrated by Nancy Willard
Don't Go Back to Sleep, poetry by Sarah Gorham
The Interlude, poetry by D.W. Fenza
Once Out of Nature, poetry by Jim Simmerman
What Happens, poetry by Robert Long
Sandcastle Seahorses, a children's story by Nikia Clark Leopold
Life in the Middle of the Century, two novellas by John Dranow
The Halo of Desire, poetry by Mark Irwin
The Eye That Desires to Look Upward, poetry by Steven Cramer
The Four Wheel Drive Quartet, a fiction by Robert Day
New World Architecture, poetry by Matthew Graham
The Maze, poetry by Mick Fedullo
Keeping Still, Mountain, poetry by John Engman
On My Being Dead and Other Stories, by L.W. Michaelson
The Intelligent Traveler's Guide to Chiribosco,
a novella by Jonathan Penner